DATE DUE

By Larry Kramer

FICTION

Faggots

PLAYS

Sissies' Scrapbook
The Normal Heart
Just Say No
The Destiny of Me

SCREENPLAY

Women in Love

NONFICTION

Reports from the holocaust:
the making of an AIDS activist

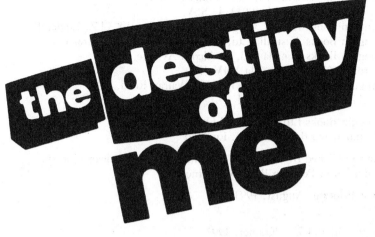

the destiny of me

A Play in Three Acts
by
Larry Kramer

A PLUME BOOK

PLUME
Published by the Penguin Group
Penguin Books USA Inc., 375 Hudson Street,
New York, New York 10014, U.S.A.
Penguin Books Ltd, 27 Wrights Lane, London W8 5TZ, England
Penguin Books Australia Ltd, Ringwood, Victoria, Australia
Penguin Books Canada Ltd, 10 Alcorn Avenue,
Toronto, Ontario, Canada M4V 3B2
Penguin Books (N.Z.) Ltd, 182–190 Wairau Road,
Auckland 10, New Zealand

Penguin Books Ltd, Registered Offices:
Harmondsworth, Middlesex, England

First published by Plume, an imprint of New American Library,
a division of Penguin Books USA Inc.

First Printing, August, 1993

REGISTERED TRADE MARK—MARCA REGISTRADA

ISBN 0-452-27016-9

I would like to thank Sanford Friedman, Bill Hart, and Morgan Jenness for their invaluable dramaturgical contributions; and Dr. Suzanne Phillips, Dr. Joseph Sonnabend, Dr. Howard Grossman, Dr. Anthony Fauci, Dr. Robert Gallo, and Richard Lynn for answering my hundreds of medical questions.

L.K.

For my brother,
Arthur Bennett Kramer.

*"I guess you could have lived without me.
I never could have lived without you."*

Thank you.
I love you.

The Destiny of Me opened on October 20, 1992, at the Lucille Lortel Theater in New York City. The Circle Repertory Company (Tanya Berezin, Artistic Director) production was presented by Lucille Lortel. It had the following cast:

Cast of Characters
(IN ORDER OF APPEARANCE)

NED WEEKS	*Jonathan Hadary*
NURSE HANNIMAN	*Oni Faida Lampley*
DR. ANTHONY DELLA VIDA	*Bruce McCarty*
ALEXANDER WEEKS	*John Cameron Mitchell*
RICHARD WEEKS	*David Spielberg*
RENA WEEKS	*Piper Laurie*
BENJAMIN WEEKS	*Peter Frechette*

Director	*Marshall W. Mason*
Sets	*John Lee Beatty*
Costumes	*Melina Root*
Lighting	*Dennis Parichy*
Original Music	*Peter Kater*
Sound	*Chuck London & Stewart Werner*

Production Stage Manager	*Fred Reinglas*

Originally produced in association with	*Rodger McFarlane and Tom Viola*

Place: Just outside Washington, D.C.
Time: Autumn, 1992.

About the Production

As with all plays, I hope there are many ways to design *The Destiny of Me*.

The original New York production turned out to be much more elaborate than I'd conceived it in my head as I wrote it. As I worked with the director, Marshall Mason, I began to fear I'd written an undesignable play (not that there should ever be such a thing!).

On *The Normal Heart* I'd had the talent of the enormously gifted Eugene Lee, ever adept at solving problems of this nature in miraculously ingenious ways, and ways that were not expensive. I suspect that Eugene's design for *The Normal Heart*—the way he solved not dissimilar problems—has been utilized unknowingly all over the world, just from the participants in one production seeing photographs of another.

This time, and it was also a great gift, I had the opportunity to work with John Lee Beatty, who'd designed many of Marshall's other productions. John Lee is another kind of theatrical genius, as obsessed with minute details as Eugene is off-the-cuff. Our set was a realistic, technical marvel, with the scenes from the past zipping in and out on clever winches. We even had a sink on stage, with running water, so that the doctors and nurses and orderlies who were constantly coming into the hospital environment could wash their hands, as they would in a real hospital.

The elaborate apparatus for the medical treatment Ned is undergoing, as well as everything having to do with blood, was also worked out meticulously. I have not, in this published version, completely detailed all this medical minutia, or the comings and goings of the nonspeaking hospital staff that the availability of a group of young Circle Rep interns allowed us to utilize in peopling our stage. Nor have I gone into too much detail about how the blood machinery looked and worked, beyond cursory descriptions.

I guess what I'm saying, and hoping, is that a lot of inventive ways will be found to deal with any problems designing and producing my play might raise—that there is no *right* way, and that, as in all theater, imagination is also one of the actors, and there are many ways to play the part.

Introduction

I began arranging for the production of *The Destiny of Me* when I thought I was shortly going to die. It's a play I've been working on for years—one of those "family" slash "memory" plays I suspect most playwrights feel compelled at some point to try their hand at in a feeble attempt, before it's too late, to find out what their lives have been all about. I figured it would be the last words of this opinionated author.

Not only did I think my play would be done while I was on my deathbed or after, I decided I would definitely leave word that it would not be done while my mother, who is now approaching ninety-three, was still alive. I certainly didn't want to be around to discover how she would react to the portrayal, by her fifty-seven-year-old homosexual son, of some fifty years of *her* life.

As destiny would have it, I appear to have received a respite from my expected imminent demise, at least one sufficient enough to ask myself: what have I gone and done?

I call *The Destiny of Me* a companion play to the one I wrote in 1985, *The Normal Heart*, about the early years of AIDS. It's about the same leading character, Ned Weeks, and the events of the earlier play have transpired before the curtain rises on the new one; it is not necessary, as they say, to have seen one to see the other. (The deathbed play remains to be written; now I have the chance to write a trilogy.)

Oh, I've had to make a few little changes. Instead of facing death so closely, Ned Weeks now only fears it mightily. And the hospital where he'd gone to die is now the hospital where he goes to try to live a little longer.

He still tries to figure out what his life's been all about.

This play now seems very naked to me. I'm overwhelmed with questions that didn't bother me before. Why was it necessary for me to write it? Why do I want people to see it? What earthly use is served by washing so much of "the Weeks family" linen in public?

When I wrote *The Normal Heart*, I had no such qualms. I knew exactly what I wanted to achieve and there was no amount of *anything* that could repress my hell-or-high-water determination to see that play produced, to hear my words screamed out in a theater, and to hope I'd change the world.

In what possible way could *The Destiny of Me* ever change the world?

About a dozen years ago I found myself talking to a little boy. I realized the little boy was me. And he was talking back. I was not only talking to myself but this myself was a completely different individual, with his own thoughts, defenses, and character, and a personality often most at odds with his grown-up self. These conversations frightened me. It's taken me years of psychoanalysis to rid myself of just such schizophrenic tendencies.

I found myself talking to this kid more and more. I found myself writing little scenes between the two of us. I was in trouble. I was falling in love with this kid. I, who face a mirror—and the world—each day with difficulty, had found something, inside myself, to love. I found myself writing this kid's journey—one that could only complete itself in death.

I should point out that I have always hated *anything* that borders on the nonrealistic. I hate science fiction and horror movies. I do not want to see a play, be it by Herb Gardner or Neil Simon or Luigi Pirandello, in which one actor (the author) talks to himself as embodied in another actor. My life has always been too bound up in harsh realities to believe in such fantastic possibilities, theatrical or otherwise. Nor have I ever been one to write comfortably in styles not realistic, not filled with facts and figures and *truth*. (Some readers tell me my novel, *Faggots*, is about as surreal a portrayal of the gay world as could be, but it was all the real McCoy to me.)

As I wrote on, in addition to worrying about my mother's reaction, I began to taunt myself with other fears. There is only one *Long Day's Journey into Night*. There is only one *Death of a Salesman*. And a million feeble attempts to duplicate their truth and to provoke their tears. And each playwright has only one family story to tell. And only one chance to tell it. Most, if they're lucky, throw their feeble attempts in the waste basket or file them with the stuff they plan to bequeath to their alma mater or unload on the University of Texas.

I further complicated my task by determining to write a personal history: a journey to acceptance of one's own homosexuality. My generation has had special, if not unique, problems along this way. We were the generation psychoanalysts tried to change. This journey, from discovery through guilt to momentary joy and toward AIDS, has been my longest, most important journey, as important—no, more important —than my life with my parents, than my life as a writer, than my life as an activist. Indeed, my homosexuality, as unsatisfying as much of it was for so long, has been the single most important defining characteristic of my life.

As I wrote of these journeys, and as we entered rehearsals, I found myself, over and over again, learning new things no amount of analysis had taught me. The father I'd hated became someone sad to me; and the mother I'd adored became a little less adorable, and no less sad. And although I'd set out, at the least, to have my day in court, actors, those magicians, grabbed hold of my words, and what had been my characters asserted themselves, and my harsh judgments were turned around in my face! My mother and father were showing me who they were, and not the other way around.

Oh, why had I written this damn play anyway!

I'd started out wanting to write a tragedy. I'd read all sorts of books that tried to define precisely what one is, including not a few that told me I couldn't write one anymore. I think the lives that many gay men have been forced to lead, with AIDS awaiting them after the decadeslong journey from self-hate, is the stuff of tragedy. And I'd thought that the marriage my parents had was tragic, too; they could have had much better lives without each other.

But, once again, I discovered some surprising things. My younger self was very funny and spunky, and it's the me of today who, despite one hundred years of therapy, has lost resilience. As for my parents' lives, well, there is a difference between tragedy and sadness. I cannot bring myself to see my father as Willy Loman. Nor my mother as Medea or Clytemnestra or Antigone or Phèdre. Or Mary Tyrone. Or Joan of Arc. The stakes (pun intended) just weren't the same.

So was my determination to see this play produced a desire for vengeance? For blame? For catharsis? Was it only hubris? (Anita Brookner enunciated many writers' main motivation in the very title of one of her own books, *Look at Me*.)

I discovered long ago that writing doesn't bring catharsis. Writing *The Normal Heart* did not release my anger or make me hate Ed Koch and Ronald Reagan less or alter the present sorry state of the AIDS plague for the better. Writing *Faggots* did not find me true love or make me any more lovable or, so far as I can see, start any mass migration by the gay community to monogamous relationships. No, getting things off your chest doesn't get them off for very long.

Carole Rothman, the artistic director at Second Stage in

New York, herself a parent, said she was uncomfortable about doing a play that "blamed" parents. (Joe Papp said he wouldn't put on any play where a father hit a son. I always thought this said more about Joe than my play.) "Blame" began to be a word that haunted me. Did I blame my parents? Is this what my play was saying? Over and over I reread my words. I wasn't blaming them. I was trying to understand what in their own lives made them the way they were and how this affected the lives of their children. I didn't see this as blame or vengeance.

In fact, I came to see their behavior as destined as my own. I even decided to change the play's title, which had been *The Furniture of Home* (taken from the same W. H. Auden poem as *The Normal Heart*). I don't know what sent me to Walt Whitman (beyond the desire to find my title in the words of another gay poet; I wonder now if it was as simple as one aging and physically deteriorating gay writer seeking inspiration from another), but I found myself reading and rereading his collected works. Sure enough, in "Out of the Cradle Endlessly Rocking," that haunting ode to life without love, I found what I was looking for—"the destiny of me."

Now I had a play and I had a title and I had a director— Marshall Mason. Then my leading actors, Colleen Dewhurst and Brad Davis, died. I lost my next leading man, Ron Rifkin, because of an unfortunate disagreement I had with the playwright Jon Robin Baitz. Ron, for whom Robbie wrote his greatest role, in *The Substance of Fire*, bowed out. It would be some time before Tanya Berezin of the Circle Repertory Company would read my play in March 1991 and immediately accept it. Like me by the men in my life, my play had first to have its own history of rejections: by the Public Theater (both Joe Papp and JoAnne Akalaitis), Manhattan Theatre Club, Lincoln Center, Playwrights Horizons (both André Bishop and Don Scardino), American Place Theater, Second

Stage, Long Wharf in New Haven, Hartford Stage, Yale Rep (both Lloyd Richards and Stan Wojewodski, Jr.), South Coast Rep in California, the Goodman and Steppenwolf in Chicago, and Circle in the Square on Broadway.

I list these not to either tempt fate (oh, the nightmare possibility of those reviews that begin, "The numerous theaters that turned down Larry Kramer's new play were wise indeed . . .") or flaunt my rejections (*The Normal Heart*, *Faggots*, and my screenplay for *Women in Love* were originally turned down by even larger numbers), but to offer this thought to other writers, and to the little child inside that one talks to: almost more than talent you need tenacity, and an infinite capacity for rejection if you are to succeed. I still don't know where you get these even after writing this play to try to find the answer.

I guess that's what my play's about. I guess that's what my life's been about.

Not much of a message, huh? Well, maybe it's about a little more. I'll have to wait and see. Each day my family surprises me more and more. And that little boy inside me.

I'll bet you didn't expect Larry Kramer to talk like this.

I set out to make sense of my life. And I found out that one's life, particularly *after* one has written about it, doesn't make sense. *Life* doesn't make sense.

But change does. And there is no change without tenacity. And change is usually very hard. With precious few gratifications along the way to encourage you to carry on. And some change is good. And necessary. And some change must not be allowed.

This sounds more like Larry Kramer.

Yes, I can make sense out of *this*.

You may not agree, and you may not change your opinion, but you will have heard me make my case. And maybe, just maybe, you will think twice before slugging your kid tonight because he or she is gay, or you will not vote for any candidate who would allow AIDS to become a plague.

Yes, I know the possibilities are slim.

So what?

The little boy in me still believes everything is possible.

Mom, you taught me this.

And you lied.

But so does art and so does hope.

This article originally appeared in the *New York Times* Arts & Leisure section on Sunday, October 4, 1992.

O you singer solitary, singing by yourself, projecting me,
O solitary me listening, never more shall I cease
    perpetuating you,
Never more shall I escape, never more the reverberations,
Never more the cries of unsatisfied love be absent from me,
Never again leave me to be the peaceful child I was before
    what there in the night,
By the sea under the yellow and sagging moon,
The messenger there arous'd, the fire, the sweet hell within,
The unknown want, the destiny of me.

From "Out of the Cradle Endlessly Rocking"
WALT WHITMAN

ACT ONE

(NED WEEKS, *middle-aged, enters a hospital room with his suitcase.*)

NED: I grew up not far from here. The trees were just being chopped down. To make room for Eden Heights. That's where we lived. That's what they named places then.

(HANNIMAN, *a nurse, pushes in a cart with medical stuff on it, including* NED's *records. She is black.*)

HANNIMAN: The eleventh floor is our floor—Infectious Diseases. We ask that you don't leave this floor, or the hospital, or the Institute's grounds, or indeed go to any other floor, where other illnesses are housed. Dr. Della Vida says it's better to have you on our side. I tell him you're never going to be on our side. You're not here to cause some sort of political ruckus? Are you?

NED: (*Unpacking some books.*) What better time and place to read *The Magic Mountain*?

HANNIMAN: Are you?

NED: I'm here for you to save my life. Is that too political?

(DR. ANTHONY DELLA VIDA *enters. He is short, dynamic, handsome, and very smooth, a consummate bureaucrat. He beams hugely and warmly embraces* NED.)

TONY: Hello, you monster!

NED: I never understand why you talk to me...

TONY: I'm very fond of you.

NED: ...after all I say about you.

HANNIMAN: "Dr. Della Vida runs the biggest waste of tax-payers' money after the Defense Department." In the Washington *Post*.

TONY: No, in the Washington *Post* he compared me to Hitler.

HANNIMAN: No, that was in the *Village Voice*. And it was "you fucking son-of-a-bitch of a Hitler."

TONY: Where was it he accused me of pulling off the biggest case of scientific fraud since laetrile?

NED: *Vanity Fair*.

TONY: (*Studying* NED's *file*.) All your numbers are going down pretty consistently. You didn't listen to me when you should have.

NED: Ah, Tony, nobody wants to take that shit.

TONY: They're wrong.

NED: It doesn't work.

TONY: Nothing works for everybody.

NED: Nobody believes you.

TONY: Then why are you here?

NED: I'm more desperate. And you sold me a bill of goods.

TONY: You begged me you were ready to try anything.

NED: I asked you when you were going to strike gold with *something*. You've spent two billion dollars.

TONY: No, sir! You asked me if I had anything I would take if I were you.

NED: No, sir! You said to me, "I've got it." And I said, "The cure!" And you said, "If you quote me I'll deny it." You slippery bastard.

TONY: You're the slippery bastard!

HANNIMAN: Yep, he sure is on our side.

NED: (*Reading from a newspaper clipping.*) "Dr. Della Vida has discovered a method to suppress the growth of the virus in mice by 80–90%..." The *New York Times*.

TONY: For over a decade you have mercilessly condemned that newspaper's coverage of this illness. Suddenly they're your experts?

NED: (*Another clipping.*) "...reconstituted genes will be introduced in transfusions of the patient's own blood... cells given new genetic instructions, to self-destruct if they are infected." *The Lancet.* (*A third clipping.*) "Conclusion: The success of this theory in *in vitro* experiments, followed by the successful inoculation of three West African sooty mangabey monkeys, leads one to hope that human experimentation can commence without further delay." The *New England Journal of Monkeys*. I'll be your monkey.

HANNIMAN: Don't say that. We have to guarantee each chimp a thirty-thousand-dollar retirement endowment. Their activists are better than your activists.

TONY: How have you been feeling? (*Starts examining* NED.)

NED: Okay physically. Emotionally shitty. We've lost.

TONY: You *are* depressed. That's too bad. You've been very useful.

HANNIMAN: Useful?

TONY: All your anger has kept us on our toes.

HANNIMAN: They have yelled at, screamed at, threatened, insulted, castigated, crucified every person on our staff. In every publication. On every network. From every street corner. Useful?

NED: Who is she? I've been infected for so long, and I still don't get sick. What's that all about? Everyone thinks I *am* sick. Everyone around me *is* sick. I keep waiting *to* get sick. I don't know why I'm *not* sick. All my friends are dead. I think I'm guilty I'm still alive.

TONY: Not everybody dies in any disease. You know that. Your numbers could even go back up on their own. Why is my hospital surrounded by your army of activists? Am I going to be burned at the stake if I can't restore your immune system?

NED: I'm not so active these days.

TONY: You?

NED: (*Softly.*) They don't know I'm here.

HANNIMAN: Why don't I believe that?

NED: What have we achieved? I'm here begging.

(NED *suddenly reaches out and touches* TONY's *face.* HANNIMAN's *back is turned.*)

This new treatment—you can't even stick it into me legally. Can you?

TONY: Ned—I do think I'm on to something. You've really got to keep your mouth shut. You've got to promise me. And then you've got to keep that promise.

NED: The world can't be saved with our mouths shut.

TONY: Give me lessons later.

NED: How long can you keep me alive? I've got work to finish. Two years. Can you do that?

TONY: You know there aren't any promises. Two years, the way you look now, doesn't seem impossible.

NED: How about three? It's a very long novel. Why are you willing to do this for me?

HANNIMAN: Because if it works, you'll scream bloody murder if anyone stands in his way. Because if it doesn't work, you'll scream bloody murder for him to find something else. That's *his* reasoning. Now *I* would just as soon you weren't here. Period.

TONY: (*To* HANNIMAN.) Give him the double d.d.b.m. (*Leaves.*)

NED: What's a double d.d.b.m.?

(*From the cart,* HANNIMAN *wields an enormous needle.* ALEXANDER, *a young boy, is seen dimly on the side. He's wet from a shower, and wrapped in towels. He comes closer to see what's going on.*)

HANNIMAN: Mice and chimps were easy. You're our first one who can talk back. Drop your drawers and bend over.

ALEXANDER: What's she doing?

NED: I want my Mommy.

ALEXANDER: Mommy's not home yet.

HANNIMAN: You even wrote in *The Advocate* you'd heard I was a lesbian.

NED: You're Mrs. Dr. Della Vida?

(*She rams the hypodermic into his ass.*)

(*Screams.*) We consider that a compliment!

ALEXANDER: Why are you here? (*No answer.*) Please tell me what's happening!

HANNIMAN: (*Still injecting him.*) I think it takes great courage for you to set foot anywhere near here. My husband works twenty hours a day and usually sleeps the other four in one of these rooms. I'm pregnant and I don't know how. Or why. With the number of patients we're seeing, I'm bearing an orphan. (*Extracts the hypodermic and takes a larger one.*)

NED: That wasn't it?

(*She laughs. She administers the second needle even deeper. He screams again, louder.*)

ALEXANDER: Tell me what's going on!

NED: I'm starring in this wonderful play about euthanasia.

(HANNIMAN *finishes and leaves.*)

ALEXANDER: Where's Benjamin? Where's *anyone?* Don't you have any friends? At a time like this? Something awful's happening. Isn't it? (*No answer.*) Will you give me a hug?

NED: Get lost, Lemon.

ALEXANDER: Just remember—*I* was here. (*Leaves.*)

NED: (*Changing from his street clothes.*) What do you do when you're dying from a disease you need not be dying from? What do you do when the only system set up to save you is a pile of shit run by idiots and quacks? What do you do when your own people won't unite and fight together to save their own lives? What do you do when you've tried every tactic you can think of to fight back and none of them has worked and you are now not only completely destitute of new ideas but suddenly more frightened than you've been before that your days are finally and at last more numbered and finite and that an obit in the *New York Times* is shortly to be yours? Why, you talk yourself into believing the quack is a genius (*Massages his sore ass.*) and his latest vat of voodoo is a major scientific breakthrough. And you check yourself in. So, here I am. At the National Institutes of Quacks.

They still don't know how this virus works inside our bodies. They still don't know how this disease progresses and what really triggers this progression. They still don't know if the virus could be hiding someplace else—its major home might not even be in the blood at all. Finally, in total desperation, my kids out there prepared a whole long list of what they still don't know; we even identified the best scientists anywhere in the world to find the answers.

When we were on the outside, fighting to get in, it was easier to call everyone names. But they were smart. They invited us inside. And we saw they looked human. And that makes hate harder.

It's funny how everyone's afraid of me. And my mouth. And my temper. They should only know I can't get angry now to save my soul. Eight years of screaming at one idiot to wake up and four more years of trying to get another idiot to even say the word can do that. They knew we couldn't keep up the fight and that eventually they'd be able to kill off all the faggots and spics and niggers. When I started yelling, there were forty-one cases of a mysterious disease. Now a doctor at Harvard is predicting a billion by the new century. And it's still mysterious. And the mystery isn't why they don't know anything, it's why they don't *want* to know anything.

So what does all this say about the usefulness of... anything?

Yes, the war is lost.

And I'd give anything to get angry again.

ALEXANDER: (*Reappearing, still wrapped in towel.*) You are not going to die!

NED: Go away.

ALEXANDER: If you die I die!

NED: Please go away.

ALEXANDER: I kept you alive for quite some time, thank you very much!

NED: Lemon—get the fuck out of here.

ALEXANDER: I was here first! Are you rich and successful and famous? Two of them? One? Did you fall in love? (*No answers.*) Every single second of my entire life I've wanted there to be somebody! I gave you great stuff to work with. How did you fuck it up? Excuse me for saying so, but I think you're a mess.

(*He goes to his Eden Heights bedroom. The walls are plastered with theatrical posters from hit shows—*South Pacific, Mister Roberts, A Streetcar Named Desire, The Glass Menagerie.)

(*To* NED *and the audience.*) Alexander the Great ruled the entire known world, from east to west and north to south! He conquered it, with his faithful companions. He was very handsome. He was very fearless. Everybody knew who he was and everybody loved him and worshiped him and cherished him. He was king of everything! (*Singing.*) "Give me some men who are stouthearted men who will fight for the right they adore!" Good evening, Mr. Murrow. Thank you for coming into my home. This is where I wrote my Pulitzer Prize play and this, of course, is where I practiced my Academy Award–winning performance. An Alexander can be anything he wants to be! Dressed up for battle in shining armor and a helmet and plumes, or a gorgeous purple royal cloak. (*Singing.*) "Who cares if my boat goes upstream, Or if the gale bids me go with the river's flow? I drift along with my fancy, Sometimes I thank my lucky stars my heart is free—And other times I wonder where's the mate for me?" (*Speaking dialogue.*) "Hello."

NED: "How do you do? Are you an actress?"

ALEXANDER: "Oh, no. But I'd give anything if I could be."

NED: "Why?"

ALEXANDER: "Because you can make believe so many wonderful things that never happen in real life." (*Singing.*) "The game of just supposing is the sweetest game I know, Our dreams are more romantic, Than the world we see."

NED: (*Singing.*) "And if the things we dream about, Don't happen to be so..."

ALEXANDER: "That's just an unimportant tech-ni-cality." *Show Boat* was the first show I saw on Broadway. (*Singing.*) "Only make believe I love you..."

NED: "Only make believe that you love me..." Oh, get dressed. Before Pop catches you.

ALEXANDER: I can be Henry Fonda in *Mister Roberts* or Cornelia Otis Skinner in *Lady Windermere's Fan*. The second balcony of the National Theater is only ninety cents and I go every other week when they change the show. I can be Ezio Pinza or Mary Martin in *South Pacific*. "One dream in my heart. One love to be living for…" And I am performing on the biggest stage and everyone is applauding me like crazy. (*Bowing.*) Thank you. Thank you very much. Oh, Ned! Nobody I know is interested in what I'm interested in. And I'm not interested in what they're interested in.

NED: And you're never going to be able to accept or understand that.

ALEXANDER: Do you get in trouble when you try to find out things?

NED: Only if you're nosey.

ALEXANDER: I'm nosey.

NED: The best people are nosey.

ALEXANDER: Thank you. I ran away once. To New York. I used all my baby-sitting money. I'd see a Broadway show every day for the rest of my life. Mom traced me to Aunt Fran's just as I was leaving to see Judith Anderson in *Medea*. Ma said under no circumstances was I allowed to see a play about a mother who murders both her children.

NED: I said, Why not?

ALEXANDER and NED: Pop wants to murder me all the time.

ALEXANDER: (*Making a turban from a towel and singing.*) "I'm gonna wash that man right out-a my hair, And send him on his way."

(*Sounds of* RICHARD WEEKS *coming home.*)

My God, Pop's home! (*Furiously getting dressed,* NED *helping him.*) I always say Hope for the Best and Expect the Worst. Ned, Alexander means Helper and Defender of All Mankind. Why'd you change my name?

NED: Alexander the Great died very young.

(RICHARD WEEKS *enters. He is almost the same age* NED *is now, but he looks much older. He is impeccably dressed. He puts down his newspaper and takes off his jacket and tie and cufflinks and rolls up his shirtsleeves. He keeps on his vest with its gold chain that holds his Phi Beta Kappa and Yale Law Journal keys. He comes across some of* ALEXANDER'*s comic books.*)

RICHARD: Come here, you!

ALEXANDER: (*From his room.*) I'm not home from school yet!

RICHARD: I warned you if I caught you buying comic books one more time I'd take away your allowance. You'll never get into Yale.

ALEXANDER: I'm going to go to Harvard.

RICHARD: You are not going to go to Harvard.

ALEXANDER: (*To* NED.) What am I supposed to say? Poppa, this strange man who lives down the block *gives* me the comic books. If I let him stick his finger up my tushie and suck my penis. He says he's in medical school and I'm helping him learn. Isn't it all right to have comic books if I don't spend my own money on them?

NED: Mordecai Rushmore.

ALEXANDER: Why do I have to lie? (*Entering, dressed.*) Hi, Pop. What's a penis? (*Grabbing the offending comic books.*)

RICHARD: (*Leaving to wash up.*) Look it up in the dictionary.

ALEXANDER: It isn't in the dictionary.

RICHARD: Then ask your mother. (*Exits.*)

HANNIMAN: (*Enters with a large bottle of pills.*) Take two of these every two hours. You have a watch. I won't have to remind you.

NED: (*As* ALEXANDER *stuffs the comics behind a book on a shelf.*) What are you doing?

ALEXANDER: I always hide them here.

NED: (*Reading the book's spine.*) Psychopathia Sexualis by Dr. Richard von Krafft-Ebing.

HANNIMAN: There seem to be more and more unusually dressed people gathering outside. What are they going to do?

NED: Look, can we please try and be friends?

ALEXANDER: Hey! I think if you're going to be with me, you really should be with me.

NED: I'm sorry if I upset you.

HANNIMAN: You're not sorry. You're scared shitless. (*Leaves.*)

RENA'S VOICE: Somebody please help me!

(RENA WEEKS *manages to open the front door, carrying large bags of groceries. She is in her forties. She wears a Red Cross uniform —skirt, jacket, and hat.*)

ALEXANDER: (*Helping her.*) Hi, Mom. Dad says to ask you what's a penis.

RENA: I told you.

ALEXANDER: Tell me again.

RENA: When you grow up, you'll insert it into the woman's sexual organ, which is called the vagina. The penis goes into the vagina and deposits semen into my uterus, and, if it's the right time of the month, pregnancy occurs, resulting, nine months later, in a child.

ALEXANDER: That's all?

RENA: What else would you like?

(RICHARD *returns, drying his hands on a towel, which he then puts around his neck. The telephone starts to ring.*)

RICHARD: Why are you so late?

RENA: You want to eat, don't you? Can't anyone else ever answer the phone?

RICHARD: Who calls me? (*Takes out some new money, peels a bill off.*)

RENA: (*Answering the phone.*) Hello.

RICHARD: I'm raising your allowance from fifty cents to one dollar.

ALEXANDER: (*Surprised.*) Thanks, Pop.

RENA: Oh, Mrs. Noble! This is Rena Weeks, Home Service Director, Suburban Maryland Chapter American Red Cross.

RICHARD: (*Trying to give the rest of the money to* RENA.) Count it. I got a raise!

RENA: (*Taking the money and putting it down.*) Could you possibly send some of your wonderful Gray Ladies to help us out driving our paraplegic vets to the ball game this Saturday while our regular volunteers work the monthly Bloodmobile?

RICHARD: I hate it that you work.

RENA: Yes, it is hard finding volunteers now the war is almost over.

(ALEXANDER *accidentally drops some canned goods.*)

RICHARD: That table cost two hundred dollars!

ALEXANDER: One hundred and seventy-five.

RENA: Yes, some other time. (*Hangs up.*)

RICHARD: They fired fifty more. Abe Lesser and his wife moved out of their apartment in the middle of the night. Nobody heard them leave. How could anybody not hear them leave?

(ALEXANDER *sits down and reads part of* RICHARD'*s newspaper, unconsciously jiggling his leg up and down with increasing speed.* RENA *puts out a cold meal; in a hurry, she'll rush through the serving, eating, and clearing.*)

RENA: It's been a terrible day for tragedy.

RICHARD: Abe Lesser is no more a Communist than Joe DiMaggio.

RENA: We had a dreadful fire in Hyattsville.

RICHARD: I went to Yale with Abie.

RENA: Six entire families were burned out of everything they owned.

RICHARD: I don't want to hear about it.

RENA: I found shelter for all of them. Six entire families, Richard.

RICHARD: That's enough! I asked you not to talk about it.

ALEXANDER: Louella Parsons is very angry at Rita Hayworth.

RENA: (*Telling* ALEXANDER.) And I had to call a lovely young bride and break the news that her husband—he was just drafted, they didn't even have time for a honeymoon—he was killed on his very first training flight.

ALEXANDER: Louella says playing bold hussies only gets Rita into trouble.

RENA: His plane just fell from the sky.

RICHARD: Didn't you hear me!

RENA: She hadn't even started receiving his paychecks and he's dead!

ALEXANDER: Louella says she should start playing nice girls like Loretta Young.

RENA: Somebody has to take care of them!

RICHARD: And I never get a hot meal!

RENA: Oh, you do too get hot meals!

RICHARD: I like my tuna salad with egg and you know it!

RENA: I didn't have time to boil eggs!

ALEXANDER: But Rita says the bold and the brazen are the only parts they offer her.

(RICHARD *suddenly and furiously swats* ALEXANDER's *leg with his part of the newspaper.*)

What'd I do now!

RICHARD: You're boring a hole in the rug!

ALEXANDER: Four hundred dollars.

RENA: Alexander, eat.

RICHARD: Five hundred dollars!

ALEXANDER: Four hundred and forty-nine ninety-five.

RICHARD: Isn't Ben coming home again?

RENA: I don't know.

RICHARD: Four hundred and ninety-nine ninety-five! Tax, delivery, and installation. He's Alexander again?

ALEXANDER: At least seven full weeks ago I changed my name to Alexander. Alex, which I thought suited me, was only the whim of a foolish child, a mere moment in time. And Benjamin has always, *always*, preferred Benjamin. You're the only one who insists on shortening him to Ben. And no, Benjamin is not coming home. He had football practice this afternoon, tonight he puts the school paper to bed, and then he's sleeping over at one of his chums. And, *and*, he has told me confidentially that he hates eating at home. With us. Everyone fights too much. (*Salts his food vigorously.*)

RENA: He didn't say any such thing.

RICHARD: (*Slapping* ALEXANDER's *hand.*) You cannot put so much salt on everything! Do you want your stomach to fall apart when you grow up?

ALEXANDER and NED: I'll let you know when I grow up.

NED: It did.

RICHARD: (*To* NED.) What did I tell you? (*To* ALEXANDER.) Ben your bosom buddy? He doesn't even know you're alive.

ALEXANDER: He does so! (*Salts his food vigorously.*)

RICHARD: Do you see what he's doing?

RENA: Richard, please don't say things like that to the boy.

RICHARD: Am I talking to the wall?

RENA: They love each other very much. Benjamin was dying for a brother. He ran all the way to the hospital.

ALEXANDER: And when he saw me he said, "God, he's ugly. What a lemon!" Why do you always have to tell that story? (*Salts vigorously again.*)

RICHARD: I wash my hands of him. He's your son.

RENA: He's your son, too. I forgot to put any salt in, I was in such a hurry.

RICHARD: You always take his side.

RENA: There aren't any sides. We're all on the same side. We're a family.

RICHARD: Where's my Gelusil? My ulcer's acting up.

NED: Take Alka-Seltzer. It's the only thing that works for me. (*Gives* RICHARD *one.*)

ALEXANDER: Here it comes, Alexander's ulcer.

NED: Did they have Alka-Seltzer then?

RICHARD: (*Preparing it in one of* NED's *hospital cups.*) I get these pains in my gut and the doctor says there's no cure and I said, of course not, how can you be cured of your own son.

NED: Of course they had Alka-Seltzer then. Adam, Noah, Abraham, Moses—all the Jews took Alka-Seltzer.

RICHARD: You haven't shut up since the day you were born.

NED: The Jews *invented* Alka-Seltzer.

ALEXANDER: And I won't shut up until the day I die!

NED: Jesus took Alka-Seltzer.

RENA: Both of you stop it! Where did this fight come from?

ALEXANDER: (*To* RICHARD.) Why don't fights with Benjamin cause your ulcer? Why is it always Alexander's ulcer?

RENA: You fought with Benjamin?

ALEXANDER: When he won his appointment it didn't look like the war would ever be over.

RICHARD: I won't let him throw away a West Point education!

ALEXANDER: But now there's no point to West Point.

RICHARD: A war isn't over just because you say it's over.

NED: World War II ended in '45 and McCarthy was the early fifties. I'm not remembering this properly.

ALEXANDER: Yes, you are, you are! You're remembering it just fine.

NED: (*Starting to take some of the pills* HANNIMAN *left.*) I don't remember what I'm remembering.

ALEXANDER: Isn't that the point? I'll tell you when you're wrong.

NED: I'm sure you will. (*Noticing the container.*) He knows I won't take this poison! (*Pumps the nurse's bell.*)

RENA: Richard, you're going to have to work the Blood-mobile on Saturday.

RICHARD: I'll be goddamned if I'll work the Bloodmobile on Saturday or any other day.

RENA: Then you can drive the paraplegics to the ball game. Take your pick. And watch your language.

RICHARD: The Bloodmobile on Saturday, Sunday you teach at Temple, and I never get a hot meal.

RENA: Now I'm not supposed to teach at Temple? How else could we pay for Alexander to learn about the history of our people?

ALEXANDER: Don't blame that one on me.

RENA: It's bad enough living in a place where we're the only Jews. It was bad enough his not being bar mitzvahed. My mother would die if she knew.

ALEXANDER: How will she know? You made me write her how sad we all were she couldn't come all the way from L.A. to see me become a man and thank you for your generous check.

NED: (*To* RENA.) Do you know I think that was my first conscious lie?

RENA: (*To* NED.) I was only trying not to break my mother's heart.

(*Goes into her bedroom.*)

ALEXANDER: Mordecai Rushmore was my first lie.

NED: He was kind of humpy.

ALEXANDER: I don't have to tell you there are a lot of comic books hidden behind Dr. Krafft-Ebing.

NED: So you like it?

ALEXANDER: It feels good. Except when it's over. When it feels bad.

RICHARD: (*Taking the money* RENA *has left by the phone.*) I got a raise.

ALEXANDER: How could I be bar mitzvahed when I don't believe in God?

RICHARD: Why do you say things like that?

ALEXANDER: What's wrong with saying what you believe?

RICHARD: You're just an obnoxious show-off!

ALEXANDER: And you're my father!

(RICHARD *raises his hand to hit him.* ALEXANDER *moves adeptly out of the way.*)

Do you believe in God?

RICHARD: Of course I believe in God!

ALEXANDER: I don't know why. He hasn't been very good to you.

NED: (*Impressed.*) Did we learn how to fight from them?

RICHARD: Then go live in Hyattsville with those goddamned six dozen burned-out families on their goddamned training flights.

ALEXANDER: I didn't learn one thing from them! Not one goddamned thing!

NED: Then where did we come from?

ALEXANDER: We made it on our own! With lots of help from me!

HANNIMAN: (*Rushing in.*) What's wrong?

NED: (*To* ALEXANDER.) So we sprang full-grown from the head of Zeus?

HANNIMAN: Are you having some sort of drug reaction?

RENA: We used to go everywhere. Mrs. Roosevelt might be there. And those Andrews Sisters.

ALEXANDER: Ma, I know all their songs!

RICHARD: I'm tired. Sometimes I feel real old, Rene.

ALEXANDER: Take *me*!

RENA: Don't say that. You'll talk yourself into it.

RICHARD: And like I'm not going to make it.

NED: (*Directed toward* RICHARD.) You're the same age I am now.

ALEXANDER: Don't you dare feel sorry for him!

RENA: You're fine and your health is fine and you finally have a full-time job. We're all fine.

NED: You have... thirty years before you die...

RENA: I feel I'm really doing something useful. I love my job.

RICHARD: Which one? You have so many.

RENA: I like helping people. Why does that bother you so? What's wrong with my feeling good? (*Starts clearing the table.*)

RICHARD: I don't feel good. I've never felt at home here. I can't wait to go back home.

NED: You can't retire for twenty years.

RICHARD: Nineteen.

NED: Amost twenty.

RICHARD: Nineteen and a half.

ALEXANDER: Nineteen and three-quarters.

RENA: (*To* ALEXANDER.) Didn't you forget something?

ALEXANDER: (*Giving her a ritual kiss.*) A kiss for the cook.

RICHARD: A kiss for the cook? What did she cook?

RENA: Washington is such a transient city. Everyone's always talking about going back to someplace else. Funny how nobody ever thinks this place is home.

ALEXANDER: We don't live *in* Washington. We live on the wrong side of the District Line. We are *of* the Capital of the United States but we are not *in* it.

RICHARD: We never should have left Connecticut. We're going back.

ALEXANDER: We are outsiders.

RENA: I like it here. People do all sorts of interesting, important things. I got a new assignment. I'm going to help avert the many accidents suffered by returning servicemen just out of military hospitals and with prosthetic limbs.

ALEXANDER: What's prosthetic limbs?

NED: (*Starts singing softly, then a little dance.*) "Blue skies, smiling at me..."

RENA: Artificial arms and legs and hands. Made of wood and metal. When these wounded men go into stores, the sales personnel recoil in fear and horror. I'm going to be trained at the Pentagon! And then I'll be sent to department stores like Garfinkel's and specialty stores, like Rich's Shoes. And I'll bring these arms and hands and legs with me so the staff can see and feel them and then they won't be so frightened of them and they can come right up to these men and say, "May I help you, sir?"

ALEXANDER: Mom, that's very depressing. I know all the Andrews Sisters' songs!

RICHARD: That's very depressing.

ALEXANDER: Please!

(RENA *goes back into her bedroom.* ALEXANDER *begins to sing a medley of Andrews Sisters' songs.*)

"Oh give me land lots of land under starry skies above..." "Drinking rum and Coca-Cola..." "Don't sit under the apple tree with anyone else but me..." "There's going to be a hallelujah day, When the boys have all come home to stay..."

RICHARD: Stop that.

ALEXANDER: (*Dancing, kicking high.*) "And a million bands begin to play..."

RICHARD: I said stop it!

ALEXANDER: "We'll be dancing the Victory Polka!"

NED: "Never saw the sun shining so bright..."

ALEXANDER: You like the way Fred Astaire dances.

RICHARD: You don't dance like Fred Astaire.

NED: "Noticing the days hurrying by..."

ALEXANDER: How do you know I won't develop? Even Fred started somewhere. "When you're in love, my how time flies..."

(RICHARD *pounces on him suddenly, trying to restrain the dance movements. But the kid refuses to stop and* RICHARD *finds himself becoming more violent than he intended.*)

Poppa!

(RICHARD *lets go, shaking his head at what has come over him; he sits down and stares into space, before taking up his paper again.*)

Why can't I do what I want to?

NED: (*Helping him up from the floor.*) That is probably the least satisfactorily answered question in the history of man.

ALEXANDER: (*Defiantly.*) Oh, I am going to do with my life every single thing I want to do I don't care what and you better, too!

(RENA *comes out wearing an outfit for hostessing at the Stage Door Canteen. She carries a wooden leg and an arm with a metal hook. She takes* NED's *hand and makes him touch the limbs.*)

RENA: I want my son to become a leader in the fight against discrimination and prejudice. Don't stay up too late. (*Unloads the limbs on* NED *and kisses him good night. Starting out, passing* RICHARD.) Last chance. It will cheer you up. (*Leaves.*)

RICHARD: Yes, I have a good job. Yes, the government is a good employer that'll never fire me if I keep my mouth shut.

(NED *gives the limbs to* ALEXANDER.)

(*Laying out utensils, bowl, and cereal for his breakfast.*) I supervise the documentation of all the ocean-going vessels that come anywhere near or leave our shores. I verify their seaworthiness. I study their manifests and any supporting documents. Then I make a decision. Yes or No. There's not much evidence of crime on the high seas anymore, so usually there isn't any reason to say No. Each day is like the one before. Each week and month and year are the same. For this I went to Yale and Yale Law School. For this I get up every day at dawn while everyone's asleep. So I can go through life stamping papers Yes. I got a raise.

ALEXANDER: So did I. Thank you, Poppa. (*Tries to hug him, still holding the limbs.*) Poppa, would you like me to get up early and have breakfast with you?

RICHARD: (*Taking the limbs from him and moving away.*) That's okay. You finish your homework, boy?

ALEXANDER: Yes, Poppa.

RICHARD: That's good. You've got to get into Yale. Good night, boy.

ALEXANDER: Good night, Poppa. Poppa...

(ALEXANDER *wants to kiss him and be kissed. But* RICHARD *goes into his bedroom, taking the limbs.*)

Does the fighting stop someday?

NED: No.

ALEXANDER: Does any dream come true? (*No answer.*) Should I stop wishing?

NED: (*Pause.*) A few dreams do.

ALEXANDER: You had me worried.

NED: Not many.

ALEXANDER: Are you afraid if you tell me the truth I'll slit my wrists?

NED: I wish you could know now everything that happened so you could avoid the things that hurt.

ALEXANDER: Would I do anything differently?

NED: I don't know if we can.

ALEXANDER: Then don't tell me. I guess it wouldn't be much fun anyway if I knew everything in advance. It *will* become fun... ? Oh, Ned, I want a friend so bad... ly!

NED: I know.

ALEXANDER: (*Taking out Dr. Krafft-Ebing and reading from it.*) "X, a young student in North Germany, began his sexual life in his thirteenth year when he became acquainted with another boy. From that point, he frequently indulged in *immissio penis in os*, although his ambition was always *penem viri in anum*. My advice was to strenuously combat these impulses, perform marital duties, eschew masturbation, and undergo treatment." You sort of get the feeling that, whatever it is, Dr. Krafft-Ebing doesn't want you to do it. Ned, who am I? Who can tell me?

NED: There isn't anyone.

ALEXANDER: I'll talk to Benjamin! Why haven't I done it before?

NED: (*Trying to hold him back.*) Alexander...

ALEXANDER: Let go!

NED: Don't tell Ben!

ALEXANDER: Benjamin is the most important person in my life.

NED: Not yet. You're not good friends yet.

ALEXANDER: We are too! Don't you say that too!

(The lights change to nighttime. There is moonlight. BENJAMIN, *in a West Point uniform and carrying a small duffel bag, comes home.* BENJAMIN *rarely raises his voice; his anger is inside of him and his quiet and serious determination is pervasive.)*

NED: Ben, you were so handsome.

*(*HANNIMAN *enters and turns on the light, breaking the mood. She carries a tray on which are four plastic cups, each with a different-colored liquid.)*

HANNIMAN: Before we extract your blood and process it to insert the necessary genetic material, we must determine if you are capable of being transfected—that is, hospitable to receiving our retroviruses containing new genetic instructions without becoming infected or infectious. Each colored liquid contains a different radioactive antibody tracer which will be able to locate that part of your declining immune system that will be the best host for our new virus. L'chaim. *(Handing him each glass and seeing that he empties each one completely.)* I thought you should know, since of course you don't, that those picketers outside, who, of course, aren't in any way connected with your being here, are growing in number. They have sleeping bags and seem to be camping out. Is something going to happen in the morning that's awful? Last year a bunch sneaked in and chained themselves to Tony's lab tables. The police had to saw off the metal legs before they could take them to jail. OMB charged our budget $300,000 for new tables so we have $300,000 less to save your life. *(As* NED *finishes by taking his pills.)* What a good boy. Now we'll be able to see if a straight path can be cleared. *(Turns out the light and leaves.)*

*(*BENJAMIN *crosses in the dark and turns on a light in the bedroom.* ALEXANDER *wakes up and throws himself into his arms.)*

ALEXANDER: Benjamin! I must talk to you! When you're not here, I talk to you from my bed to yours. Do you talk to me? (*No answer.*) I pretend Mom and Pop are both dead in a car crash and you and I live together happily ever after.

BENJAMIN: Hey, cheer me up, Lemon.

ALEXANDER: Guess what I got voted in class? (*No answer.*) Most talkative. (*No answer.*) Oh, Benjamin, I have so much to say. It's imperative I talk to you.

(RICHARD, *in pajamas and slippers, enters, pulling on a robe.* RENA, *in nightgown and slippers only, follows, bearing a plate of brownies.*)

BENJAMIN: I'd hoped you, not Uncle Leon, would be there for my pretrial deposition. Not as my lawyer. As my father.

RICHARD: I almost died!

BENJAMIN: My trial was scheduled long before your operation. Your operation wasn't an emergency. I was court-martialed.

RICHARD: I had to go when the doctor was free.

RENA: He's very famous.

BENJAMIN: Uncle Leon showed up three days late. They put me in detention until he came. The first thing he said to me was: "Your Daddy has more money to pay for a lawyer than you think." You went to Uncle Leon, after not talking to him all these years, so you wouldn't have to pay for a lawyer?

RICHARD: I don't know anything about the kind of law that governs the trouble you're in!

BENJAMIN: What else is there to know when your own son says he's innocent?

ALEXANDER: Benjamin, I must talk to you.

NED: He really does have something important in his own life right now. Try and understand.

RICHARD: How did you plead?

BENJAMIN: Not guilty.

RICHARD: I didn't expect you to listen to me. (*Pause.*) I almost died. Did you know that?

BENJAMIN: That's why I'm here. They don't just let you out of beast barracks. How do you feel?

RICHARD: They cut out my insides. I had a hemorrhage. I almost bled to death.

RENA: Then the nurse left a window open and he got pneumonia. There was a sudden summer storm. By the time we finally got back here this room was flooded. Alexander and I got down on our hands and knees and sopped up water all night.

BENJAMIN: If either of you has any notions of my staying at West Point, please disabuse yourselves of them immediately. Ma, please put on a robe.

RENA: That's very thoughtful of you, darling. (*To* ALEXANDER.) Get me my robe.

(ALEXANDER *rushes in and out so he won't miss anything.*)

RICHARD: Why are you deliberately choosing to fight the system!

BENJAMIN: Where do you find choice? I'm accused of turning my head all of two inches during a dress parade because the man next to me tripped. For this a lieutenant colonel, a major, a captain, eight cadets have spent two months haggling over whether it was really four inches instead of two inches. But in reality I lose a year of my life not because I turned my head at all but because my drill inspector, Lieutenant Futrell, hates Jews.

RICHARD: That's right. They don't like Jew boys. Why do you want to make so much trouble?

BENJAMIN: Why do you take their side?

RICHARD: It's your word against theirs.

BENJAMIN: He lied.

RICHARD: Yes, he called you a liar.

BENJAMIN: He called me a kike. At four-thirty in the morning, I was pulled out of my bed, and hauled naked out into the snow by a bunch of upperclassmen, and forced to stand up against a brick wall, which was covered with ice...

ALEXANDER: Poor Benjamin.

RENA: Such a good education going to waste.

BENJAMIN: Please stop saying things like that.

RICHARD: Can't you see how impossible it is to be the only one on your side?

BENJAMIN: Can't you see I don't mind being the only one on my side?

ALEXANDER: Neither do I! (*As* RICHARD *is about to turn on him.*) Why can't you believe my brother!

BENJAMIN: Thanks, boy. I guess it was too much to expect I'd have the support of my parents.

RENA: Don't say that.

BENJAMIN: Why not? You're asking me to say I'm guilty, when I'm not, and to allow such black marks to enter my permanent record, and to carry on as if nothing has happened. The only thing that keeps me going is some inexplicable sense of my own worth and an intense desire not to develop the habit of quitting.

NED: Where did we come from, Ben?

ALEXANDER: He's magnificent!

RICHARD: Go to bed!

ALEXANDER: Never!

BENJAMIN: I am going to *force* them into declaring me guilty or innocent. They will be compelled to disprove the validity of my word.

ALEXANDER: It's the only way.

BENJAMIN: And unless you are willing to back up my judgment, we shall be coming to a parting of the ways.

ALEXANDER: (*To* NED.) How can he not help me?

RICHARD: I thought you came home to see me because I almost bled to death. (*Starts to leave, then turns.*) My own brother! We were going to be partners for life. He threw me out at the height of the Depression. Your mother says I quit because he made my life so miserable that I had no choice but to resign. Her and her peculiar version of the truth. My own brother fired me! I loved him and looked up to him like he was God and that's what he did. Your

Mom and I couldn't afford the rent so we had to default on our lease and move to someplace cheaper and Leon, for some reason I could never understand, buys up the remainder of that apartment's lease and twenty years later when Mom dies and leaves her few bucks to me, Leon, my brother, sues me for the $3000 back rent we didn't have in our pocket to pay plus interest for the twenty years. What kind of brother is that? We were going to be partners for life. Yes, I sent for him to help save you in your troubles. He has connections in high places that I'll never have. He's the best lawyer I know, the best lawyer I ever knew and ever will. Even if I don't talk to him. (*Leaves.*)

RENA: (*Kissing* BENJAMIN *good night.*) Everything will be fine. (*Kissing* ALEXANDER *good night.*) I love you both very much. (*Picking up plate and offering brownies.*) I made your favorites. I warned him Grandma Sybil should have left her money equally to both her sons. The funny thing is, after Leon was paid back, all it bought me was a new winter coat. You would have thought she'd left us the Hope Diamond. There's nothing in the world my sons can't do. (*Leaves.*)

(BENJAMIN *strips down to his undershorts.* ALEXANDER *tries not to look at him, but peeks anyway.*)

ALEXANDER: Do you have a favorite song? (*No answer.*) "One dream in my heart, One love to be living for..." You're not coming home, are you?

BENJAMIN: (*Looking out the window.*) There's not much safety around. As best we can, Alexander, we've got to tough it out. I left home a long time ago.

ALEXANDER: How do I get out? (*No answer.*) "One love to be dreaming of..." Honestly, sometimes I think I live here all alone.

NED: You do.

ALEXANDER: Oh, shut up. Benjamin, I need help.

NED: Boy, you have some mouth on you.

BENJAMIN: I'm going to go to Yale. It's the surest way I know to get rich.

ALEXANDER: It didn't help Pop.

BENJAMIN: Yes, it did. He found his job down here through some classmate. He'd still be unemployed.

ALEXANDER: What am I going to do?

BENJAMIN: You'll be at Yale soon enough.

ALEXANDER: I can't wait *that* long!

BENJAMIN: You'd be better off at some small liberal-artsy place where they don't mind you being different.

ALEXANDER: (*Pause.*) You can see I'm different?

BENJAMIN: A blind man can see you're different.

ALEXANDER: (*Pause.*) How am I different? (*No answer.*) Please tell me.

BENJAMIN: Lemon, I'm in trouble. Let's get some shuteye. (*Turns out light.*)

ALEXANDER: "Close to my heart he came, Only to fly away, Only to fly as day flies from moonlight..."

(HANNIMAN *enters and yanks open the blinds, letting in the light. She has equipment for drawing blood.*)

HANNIMAN: Not a morning person? Now we take some tests. I thought you would be out there directing your troops. There are twice as many. Thousands. Speeches. Firecrackers. Bullhorns. Rockets. Red glares. Colored smoke. It actually was very pretty. Lots of men dressed up like nurses. There don't seem to be any TV cameras.

NED: That's too bad.

HANNIMAN: Isn't it. Over fifty arrests so far. Mounted police and tear gas. One of the horses crushed somebody's foot. Why don't you like my husband? Is it some sort of sin to work for the government? Do you have any idea how much work all this involves? Tony's been up all night, culturing healthy cells to mix with your unhealthy ones. Then they'll be centrifuged together so they can be put into your blood. Then, from this, additional cells will be drawn off, which then are also genetically altered, so that the infecting part is rendered harmless before it's put back into you. That's for the anti-sense part. To sort of fake out the infected cells and lead them over the cliff to their doom. If it works... Well, it's worked with a little girl with another disease. If it works on you... I don't let myself think how proud I'll be. Why don't they know out there that you're in here? (*No answer.*) Would they think you'd crossed over to the enemy? (*No answer.*) They hate us that much?

NED: Too many of us have been allowed to die.

HANNIMAN: Allowed?

NED: There's not one person out there who doesn't believe that intentional genocide is going on.

HANNIMAN: So. Their saint is now a sinner.

NED: A sinner. My late lover's ex-wife, Darlene, whom Felix hadn't seen for over fifteen years, and who had remarried immediately after their divorce an exceptionally rich man, turned up at the memorial service. She brought her own preacher from Oklahoma. Uninvited, he got up and delivered a sermon. To a church filled with hundreds of gay men and lesbians, he yelled out: "Oh, God, take this sinner, Felix Turner, for he knew not what he did." There was utter silence. Then I stood up and walked over and stood right under his nose and screamed as loud as I think I've ever screamed: "Felix Turner was not a sinner! Felix Turner was a good man! The best I ever knew."

ALEXANDER: *(Rushing in.)* Who's Felix Turner!

NED: In due course.

(ALEXANDER *withdraws.*)

Darlene drew herself up and marched right over to me and shouted even louder: "I now know that I have been placed on this earth to make you and all like you miserable for your sins." And we've been in court ever since, fighting over his will, which left everything to me. I was in love for five minutes with someone who was dying. I guess that's all I get.

HANNIMAN: *(Finishes taking blood.)* "The desires of the heart are as crooked as corkscrews."

NED: "Not to be born is the best for man." W. H. Auden.

HANNIMAN: I know.

NED: He was a gay poet.

HANNIMAN: Well, I agree with him anyway.

NED: How do you know that poem?

HANNIMAN: If I were one of your activists, I would respond to that insulting question: Go fuck yourself. But I am only a beleaguered nurse, with a B.A., an M.S., and a Ph.D., who is breaking her butt on the front lines of an endless battle, so I reply: Go fuck yourself. "This long disease, my life."

NED: Alexander Pope.

HANNIMAN: Not a gay poet.

NED: (*Taking more pills.*) These are making me sick to my stomach.

HANNIMAN: Take an Alka-Seltzer. (*Leaves.*)

ALEXANDER: (*Rushing back in.*) Did I hear you correctly? You were only in love for five minutes? That's terrible! What did you mean, That's all you get? Mommy! What's wrong with me?

(ALEXANDER *runs into her bedroom.* RENA *wears only a half-slip and is having trouble hooking her bra up in the back. He automatically hooks her up.*)

RENA: I need new brassieres. It's time to visit Aunt Leona. What's wrong?

ALEXANDER: I'm *different*! Even Benjamin says so.

RENA: Her company won't give her one extra penny from all the millions they make from her designs. They're hers! You see how impossible it is for a woman to be independent? "Different" doesn't tell me enough.

NED: Ma, why don't you put on a dress?

RENA: If you're going to become a writer, you must learn to be more precise with words.

NED: Do not sit half-naked with your adolescent son. Is that precise enough?

ALEXANDER: (*To* NED.) Why does it bother you guys so much? She does it all the time. I don't even look. (*To* RENA.) I don't want to be a writer anymore. *The Glass Menagerie* didn't win the Pulitzer Prize. Ma, how could they not know it was such a great play? They gave it to a play about a man who talks to an invisible rabbit. I'm going to be an actor.

NED: What do you mean, you don't look?

ALEXANDER: I look at Ponzo Lombardo. In gym. He's growing these huge tufts of pub-ic hair. Around his penis. Around his huge penis. Which she doesn't know how to tell me about and he tells me to look up in the dictionary.

NED: Pubic hair.

ALEXANDER: Pubic hair.

RENA: I was going to be an actress.

ALEXANDER: Around his huge penis.

NED: That you pronounced correctly.

RENA: I had an audition for a radio program. On NBC. Coast to coast.

ALEXANDER: You never told me that. What happened?

RENA: I was summoned to the station. Oh, I was so excited.

ALEXANDER: Then what happened?

RENA: I walked round and around the block.

ALEXANDER: Then what happened?

RENA: I walked around again.

ALEXANDER: You never went inside?

RENA: Benjamin was just a baby. I couldn't leave him.

NED: You were going to tell her how you feel so different.

ALEXANDER: But she could have become a star of the air-waves!

NED: She didn't become a star of the airwaves.

ALEXANDER: Mommy—isn't it a good thing... being different?

RENA: We're all different in many ways and alike in many ways and special in some sort of way. What are you trying to tell me?

ALEXANDER: Is it okay for me to... marry a... for instance... colored girl?

NED: Oh, for goodness' sake.

RENA: You know how important it is for Jewish people to marry Jewish people. There are many famous Jews—Jascha Heifetz and Dinah Shore and Albert Einstein and that baseball player your father's so crazy about, Hank Whatshisname. But we can't name them out loud.

ALEXANDER: Why not?

RENA: If they know who we are, they come after us. That's what Hitler taught us, and Senator McCarthy is teaching us all over again.

ALEXANDER: What if I find a colored girl who's Jewish?

(*She puts her hand to his forehead to see if he has a fever.*)

(*Breaking away.*) All I know is I feel different! From as long ago as I remember! You always taught me to be tolerant of *everyone*. You did mean it, didn't you? I *can* trust you?

RENA: Give me an example of what makes you think you're different.

ALEXANDER: I don't ever want to get married.

RENA: Of course you do. Everyone gets married. That's what you do in life. You get married. You fall in love with someone wonderful and you get married.

ALEXANDER: Are you really happy with Daddy?

RENA: Than with whom?

ALEXANDER: Cary Grant.

RENA: I never met Mr. Grant.

ALEXANDER: He's gorgeous.

RENA: Alexander, gorgeous is... well, it's a word that's better for me than for you.

ALEXANDER: Why can't I say gorgeous?

RENA: It's too... effusive for a man, too generous.

ALEXANDER: What's wrong with being generous? You would have been happier with Cary Grant, too. We could all have lived happily ever after in Hollywood—you and me and Benjamin and Cary. Why'd you settle for Richard Weeks?

RENA: Don't you think I love your father?

ALEXANDER: *I* don't.

NED: I actually said it out loud.

ALEXANDER: No, *I* said it out loud.

NED: Once again, I remind you, this is not what you set out to talk about.

ALEXANDER: But doesn't it fit in nicely?

RENA: I had lots of beaux. One was very handsome. But your father took me in his arms on our very first date and looked deep into my eyes and said, You're the girl I'm going to marry.

ALEXANDER: (*Cuddling seductively close to her.*) Tell me about the handsome one.

RENA: (*Running her hand along his leg.*) You're growing up so.

NED: Please, Ma.

RENA: You never tell me how much you love me anymore. You used to tell me all the time, Mommy, I love you more than anyone and anything in the whole wide world.

ALEXANDER: (*Touched and guilty.*) Oh, Mommy, I'm grown up now and I'm not supposed to say things like that.

RENA: Oh, silly billy, who says?

ALEXANDER: Please tell me what to do!

RENA: About what!

ALEXANDER: I've got to get ready for my Halloween Pageant.

(*He breaks away and runs into the living room, where he opens an old trunk.*)

HANNIMAN: (*Entering with medical cart.*) Now we take some blood.

(*She will take blood and put some in each of four containers.*)

NED: The straight path has been cleared?

(HANNIMAN *nods.*)

I am transfectious and not infectious?

HANNIMAN: Transfected. Now I didn't say that. That's our goal. And by all Tony's measurements and calculations, you appear to be—so far—a good candidate.

RENA: (*Pulling on a housedress and joining* ALEXANDER.) That's all that's left from when we were in Russia and they came after all the Jews and we had to run if we wanted to stay alive. You'd think they'd give us a rest. Why does someone always want someone else dead?

ALEXANDER: I'll bet the handsome one wasn't Jewish.

RENA: No, he wasn't.

ALEXANDER: What was his name?

RENA: Drew.

ALEXANDER: Drew.

RENA: Drew Keenlymore.

ALEXANDER: Drew Keenlymore! Oh! What did he do?

RENA: He was my professor.

ALEXANDER: A poor gentile.

RENA: No, he wasn't. He was from one of the oldest families in Canada and his brother was Prime Minister.

ALEXANDER: Oh, Mom! Did he take you in his arms and kiss you all over and say he wanted to marry you?

RENA: They didn't do things like that in those days.

ALEXANDER: You just said Pop did.

(*He is putting on Russian clothing from the trunk—a peasant blouse, skirt, sash, babushka, from* RENA's *youth.*)

RENA: Your Aunt Emma married a gentile. Momma wouldn't talk to her for twenty years. (*Helps him.*)

ALEXANDER: Did you love Drew?

RENA: I had long auburn hair. Everyone said I was very pretty. I had many chances.

(HANNIMAN *exits.*)

ALEXANDER: What happened to him?

RENA: I met your father.

NED: Who comes home and finds you in a dress.

RENA: No, I knew him already.

ALEXANDER: And you never saw Drew Keenlymore again. (*Stuffs Kleenex from* NED's *bedside table into the blouse to make breasts. To* NED.) Mickey Rooney did this in *Babes on Broadway.*

NED: You hate Mickey Rooney.

ALEXANDER: I'm not so crazy about Pop either.

NED: That is a motivation that had not occurred to me.

ALEXANDER: That's what we're here for, kid. (*Tosses him back the Kleenex box.*)

RENA: No. I saw him again.

ALEXANDER: You did?

RENA: He wrote me he was coming to New York. This was before you were born and Richard was still with Leon and it wasn't working out, Leon bullied Richard mercilessly, the one thing I always pray is you and Benjamin will never fight and always love each other—will you promise me?

ALEXANDER: Don't worry about that—what happened!

RENA: He took me to Delmonico's. I didn't have a nice dress.
But I dressed up as best I could. I felt like a child, going
back to my teacher, with a marriage that was in trouble, I
shouldn't be telling you all of this, I wish you could like
him more... There was no money! In the bank, in the
country. Everyone was poor, except your Uncle Leon, he
and Aunt Judith living so high off the hog, you should have
seen their apartment, in the El Dorado, with two full-time
maids. (*Gets some makeup from her vanity and puts some lipstick
and rouge on him.*)

ALEXANDER: Go back to Delmonico's.

RENA: After lunch, Drew asked me to come back to his hotel.
The Savoy Plaza.

ALEXANDER: And?

RENA: I didn't go.

ALEXANDER: Not again! Alexander Keenlymore, farewell!

RENA: I had a baby to feed.

ALEXANDER: Benjamin could have had two full-time maids!
Momma, don't you want to be different?

(RICHARD *suddenly appears, home from work, exhausted. He is
furious at what he sees.*)

RICHARD: What are you doing to him?

RENA: Don't use that tone of voice to me.

RICHARD: Look at him! He's a sissy! Your son is a sissy!

RENA: He's your son, too!

RICHARD: If he were my son, he wouldn't be wearing a dress. If he were my son, he'd come with me to ball games instead of going to your la-de-da theater. Your son is a sissy! (*Hits him.*)

RENA: Richard!

(RICHARD *hits him again.* ALEXANDER *is strangely passive.* RICHARD *corners him and can't stop swatting him.*)

Stop it!

RICHARD: Sissy! Sissy! Sissy!

NED: Why aren't you fighting back?

ALEXANDER: When he hit me last week I vowed I'd never talk to him again. (*Singing to himself.*) "Waste no time, make a switch, drop him in the nearest ditch..."

RENA: This time I won't come back when you turn up begging.

NED: Never run from a fight.

ALEXANDER: "Don't try to patch it up, Tear it up, Tear it up..."

RICHARD: That was a million years ago in another lifetime.

ALEXANDER: "You can't put back a petal when it falls from a flower..."

RENA: I can do it again!

ALEXANDER: "Or sweeten up a fella when he starts turning sour. Oh, no!..."

RENA: It's never too late to correct our mistakes.

ALEXANDER: "Oh, nooooo!"

Jonathan Hadary as Ned Weeks.

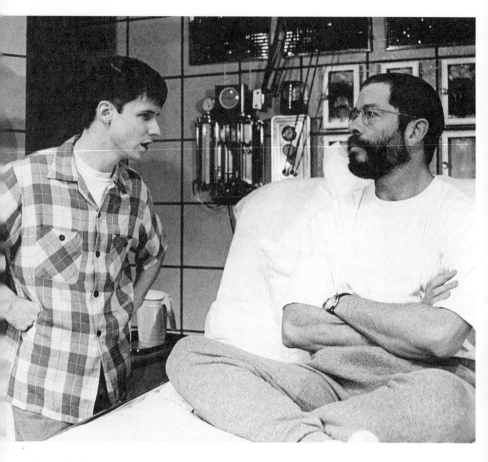

John Cameron Mitchell as Alexander Weeks (left)
with Jonathan Hadary as Ned.

From left to right, John Cameron Mitchell as
Alexander, with Piper Laurie as Rena Weeks, Peter
Frechette as Ben Weeks and Jonathan Hadary as Ned.

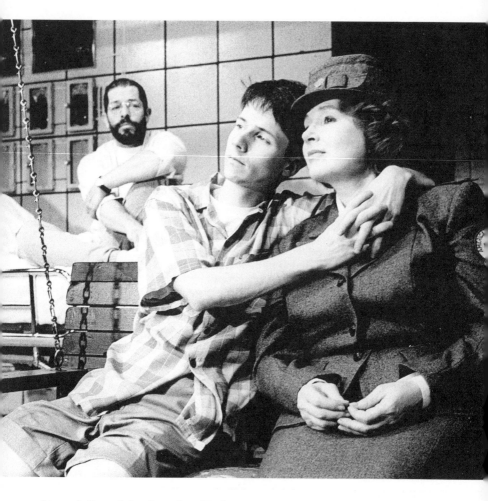

From left to right, Jonathan Hadary as Ned,
John Cameron Mitchell as Alexander and
Piper Laurie as Rena.

NED: (*To* RICHARD.) Daddy, why did you hit me?

RICHARD: You have an awful life ahead of you if you're a sissy.

NED: How do you know?

RICHARD: Everybody knows. (*To* RENA.) You want to see something? You who always defends her darling son. You want to see what he does to himself?

ALEXANDER: "If you laugh at diff'rent comics, If you root for diff'rent teams . . ."

(RICHARD *rips the skirt and underpants off him.*)

RENA: Stop tearing my dress! It's all that's left!

ALEXANDER: "Waste no time, Weep no more..."

RICHARD: I come home from the ballgame, I smell this awful smell, like something died. I caught him. Rena, I really let him have it.

(RICHARD *is trying to get ahold of* ALEXANDER'S *penis. It becomes a tussle of him almost getting it, and* ALEXANDER *evading his grasp just in time.*)

RENA: You hit him?

RICHARD: Of course I hit him!

ALEXANDER: "Show him what the door is for..."

RICHARD: He had his privates all covered up with depilatory cream!

ALEXANDER: "Rub him out-a the roll call and drum him out-a your dreams!" LET GO!

RICHARD: (*To* RENA.) Don't you even care?

RENA: I do care!

ALEXANDER: I'm the only boy in my entire class except Ponzo Lombardo who has any puberty hair and everybody laughs at him!

RICHARD: (*Starts ripping down the theater posters from the walls.*) Thank God at least I've got one son who's a man.

ALEXANDER: Don't! They're the most precious thing I have!

RICHARD: So this is what it takes to get you to talk to me.

RENA: Don't do that to the boy!

RICHARD: This is what we do to sissies.

(ALEXANDER *crawls around trying to smooth out his beloved posters and piece them back together.*)

ALEXANDER: It's Halloween! I wrote a play. Mr. Mills divided my scout troop, half into boys and half into girls. I didn't have any choice!

RICHARD: You wrote a play?

RENA: Tonight's his opening night. He invited us.

ALEXANDER: (*Screaming with all his might.*) I hate you!

RENA: Don't say that!

ALEXANDER: You taught me to always tell the truth!

NED: Go for it! (*Feels dizzy. Swallows more pills.*)

ALEXANDER: (*To* NED, *furious.*) Get me out of this!

RENA: Apologize to your father immediately!

ALEXANDER: (*To* RENA *and* RICHARD.) I hate both of you!

RICHARD: (*Really hitting him.*) Do what your mother says!

ALEXANDER: (*Grabbing the Russian shawl, stepping into women's shoes, and standing up to both of them.*) Go to hell! (*Running off, as best he can, yelling.*) Trick or treat! Trick or treat!

(HANNIMAN *rushes into the room. Her white coat is heavily bloodied.*)

HANNIMAN: Are you happy now? Look what your people did to me!

End of Act One

ACT TWO

(NED *enters in a wheelchair, singing an Andrews Sisters' song.* HANNIMAN, *in a clean white coat, wheels in a cart with a small insulated chest.* DR. DELLA VIDA *follows.* NED *carries a huge poster that reads* TONY AND GEORGE, YOU ARE MURDERING US *over big blow-ups of* DELLA VIDA *and George Bush. He holds it in front of the window, which provokes cheers from outside.*)

TONY: Why do they hate me?

HANNIMAN: These are all over the hospital. Plastered on the corridor walls, in the johns, in the cafeteria, in the Director's office. On the X-ray machines!

NED: (*Putting up the poster on a wall.*) I had my CAT scan lying under a picture of you. It was very sexy.

TONY: You wish. Get into bed.

(NED *does so.* HANNIMAN *pulls back a curtain along the wall, revealing elaborate equipment—a high-tech orgy of gleaming cylinders, dials, tubes, bells, and lights, all connected to a computer.*)

NED: This is it? Wouldn't it be easier if I just checked into a monastery and took sleeping pills?

TONY: You drown my wife in fake blood. You chop the legs off my lab tables. You've got some crazy gay newspaper up in New York that claims I'm not even studying the right virus. They call me Public Enemy Number One. Why aren't you guys proud of me? If I'm not in my lab, I'm testifying, lobbying, pressuring, I'm on TV ten times a week, I fly to conferences all over the world, I churn out papers for the journals, I supervise hundreds of scientists, I dole out research grants like I'm Santa Claus—what more do you want?

(HANNIMAN *carefully takes a sack of blood from the container and gives it to* TONY. *He inserts it into part of the machine. They repeat the procedure for two more sacks.*)

NED: A cure.

TONY: I'm not a magician.

NED: Now's not the time to tell me. There's no end in sight. That's why they hate you. You tell every reporter you have enough money. That's why they hate you. You tell Congress you have everything you need. That's why they hate you. You say more has been learned about this disease than any disease in the history of disease. That's why they hate you. You say the President cares. That's why they hate you.

(TONY *and* HANNIMAN *attach* NED *to the machine.*)

TONY: He does care! He tells me all the time how much he cares!

NED: You asked me, I told you. You're the one in charge and you're an apologist for your boss. That's why they...

TONY: If I weren't, do you think I'd get *anything*! You don't understand the realities of this town.

NED: The reality of this town is that nobody can say the word penis without blushing.

(RENA, ALEXANDER, *and* RICHARD *enter. It's evening, shadowy, at a seaside boardinghouse in Connecticut, on Long Island Sound.*)

HANNIMAN: The President named him a hero.

NED: No comment. On the grounds he might murder *me*. Wait!

TONY: (*Pulling a lever to release the blood into* NED.) This construct is the first transfect of anti-sense. Competing protein mechanisms will effect a cross-reactive anti-self.

RENA: (*Talking into a pay phone on a wall. Dropping in coins with each call.*) Jane, we've finally made it!

NED: That's what we want?

TONY: That's what we want.

RENA: Get your date book out. You're first!

TONY: If we're   , it will screw up your reproductive process.

NED: I'd assumed that already was screwed up.

TONY: Of your *viral* load.

RENA: It's been the longest year.

NED: Tell me again there isn't any down side.

TONY· I never told you there wasn't any down side.

     ou did too!

TONY· It's too late now.

ALEXANDER: (*To* NED.) Come with me.

TONY: (*Taking* NED's *hand.*) Relax.

NED: (*Grabbing* TONY.) Tony, I'm afraid.

TONY: We're going to be just fine.

RENA: Friday night at seven! Perfect! We can hardly wait! (*Hangs up, enters the engagement in her datebook.*)

ALEXANDER: Ned, come back. Only two more weeks to Yale! No more Eden Heights. My new life! We don't have much time left before I grow into you and you kick me out. (*Pulls* NED *with him.*) Come on!

(TONY *and* HANNIMAN *leave.* ALEXANDER *helps* NED, *still connected by tubes to the machinery, get out of bed and walk to sit beside* RICHARD *on a porch swing.*)

NED: (*Applying salt liberally to some food.*) Hi, Poppa.

RENA: (*To* RICHARD, *as she dials another number.*) Jane and Barney are taking us to their new country club that costs a thousand dollars a year per family just to join. (*Into phone.*) Grace, darling, this is Rena! Just this minute! Tell me when you're free!

ALEXANDER: (*To the audience.*) Every summer we come back to Connecticut for two weeks at Mrs. Pennington's Seaside Boarding House, and every year everyone Mom and Pop grew up with has become richer and richer.

(RICHARD *grabs the salt away from* NED.)

(*To* NED.) Did I say that well?

NED: First-rate. And every summer you feel more and more different.

ALEXANDER: (*To the audience.*) And every summer I feel more and more frightened. Of what I don't know.

RENA: A swim in your new pool and lobsters for luncheon! Saturday at noon. We can hardly wait! (*She hangs up, enters the engagement, checks her address book, and dials another number.*)

(NED *grabs the salt back from* RICHARD.)

Grace and Percy bought that big estate in Westport.

(RICHARD *grabs the salt back from* NED.)

Cole Porter wrote some famous song there.

(NED *grabs the salt back from* RICHARD.)

NED: I want to eat it the way I want to eat it.

RENA: Percy sold his business for a million dollars and re-tired.

RICHARD: Who's going to pay the bills when you get sick?

NED and ALEXANDER: I'll let you know when I get sick.

ALEXANDER: Tradition means a great deal in our family.

RENA: Dolores, darling, this is Rena! Quiet, both of you! Oh, my God! (*To* RICHARD.) Dolores and Nathan are going around the world for an entire year.

RICHARD: I can't take it anymore. (*To* NED.) Why are you always so ungrateful?

RENA: I've always dreamed of a trip like that.

NED: Everything you always blame me for demands I defend myself.

ALEXANDER: You're playing me really well.

RICHARD: Blame? What are you talking about? (*Grabs the salt back.*) Blame!

RENA: An informal candlelight dinner for fifty on your out-
door terrace under the stars! Saturday at nine. You'll send
a car and driver! We can hardly wait! (*Slamming down the
phone.*) I've heard this fight for the last time! This is supposed
to be a wonderful vacation! I've been on the phone calling
people I haven't seen or spoken to or heard from in a year.
Why don't you ever call them? They're your old childhood
chums, too. I feel like such a suppliant. Inviting people to
take us out and feed us. (*Having dialed another number.*) Tessie, it's Rena!

RICHARD: What I need's a vacation from him.

RENA: Are you free on Sunday?

ALEXANDER: Just two more weeks you won't ever have to see
me again.

RENA: Don't say that!

RICHARD: Maybe then I'll feel better. Where's Ben?

RENA: You think he confides in me? (*Into phone.*) A cruise on
your *yacht*? Cocktails at five to watch the sunset. We can
hardly wait. (*Hangs up.*) Tessie and Isadore have a yacht.

(NED *suddenly feels a little woozy. He stands up uncertainly. A
bell rings softly. A yellow light goes on. He indicates to a concerned*
ALEXANDER *that he should carry on. He makes his way back to
bed.*)

ALEXANDER: Benjamin is driving from New Haven in the
new secondhand Ford he bought with his own money. He
has jobs and he has scholarships and he's paying his own
way and he's free, he's a free man, ever since he beat West
Point and they said he wasn't a liar. So what do you know
what's right for him or me or anybody? He won! My
brother, whom you said wouldn't win, won!

(RICHARD *is standing directly in front of him.* ALEXANDER *holds his ground.* RICHARD *turns and leaves.*)

RENA: Who.

ALEXANDER: Who. (*Trying to kiss* RENA.) A kiss for the cook. (*As she pointedly ignores him.*) Now, Alexander, you know I don't like it when you talk back to your father like that. Yes, Momma, I know. I know you didn't mean it, dear. But I did mean it, Momma. Oh, boy, did I mean it. And I don't think I did anything wrong. Well, you can do your Mom a great big favor. Even if you don't mean it. Just do it for me. For the Mommy you love. I will not apologize! Ever!

(*The yellow light goes off.*)

RENA: You used to say, Mommy, I'll do anything you ask me.

ALEXANDER: Ma, every kid says that.

RENA: Oh, do they? What else do they say?

NED: Mommy, I am going to become so famous someday, just so I can get away from here!

RENA: My last case before we left was a family without a father. They lived in a shack. The lovely young mother. With two adorable children. Who threw up all over the house. And bled all over the sheets. From some strange illness.

NED: And I must never forget that those two diseased babies might have been me and Benjamin.

RENA: The point is we're all healthy and together and he loves you very much.

NED: The point is in my entire life I never believed for one single minute that my father ever loved me. The point is I can't even figure out if I've ever been loved at all.

(ALEXANDER *is troubled by this*.)

RENA: The point is I love him and I love you and he loves me and he loves you and we all love each other very very much!

(ALEXANDER *goes to sit on the swing*.)

I was so proud, being asked to be an official hostess. But you didn't dance with your own mother at your own graduation prom, not once.

ALEXANDER: Nobody danced with their *mother!*

RENA: Bernie Krukoff did. Neil Nelson did. Skipper with the red hair did. Do you know how much I wanted you? Do you? Mr. Know-It-All. You think you know it all. Some things you don't know.

ALEXANDER: You told me about Drew Keenlymore.

RENA: I did not.

NED: You did, too.

ALEXANDER: Before I found his letters.

RENA: I don't even know where they are.

NED: Hidden in a navy crocheted purse inside an old Macy's hatbox at the back of the top of your bedroom closet, over on the far right.

ALEXANDER: The purse is cable stitch.

RENA: Your great-grandmother crocheted that purse. She was married three times and she divorced each one of them.

She traveled all over the world. And then she came home and my Poppa took care of her until the day she died. She was ninety-nine. She was one gutsy lady.

NED: She was one scary lady. Always reading her Bible out loud, day and night, and barking orders in Hebrew.

ALEXANDER: Grandma Sybil was the scary one!

RENA: (*Sitting between them.*) After we got married, your Grandmother Sybil made Daddy promise he'd never leave her, that one of her sons would always look out for her. Richard kept his promise, which is why she left him the money. He worshiped her. Her great sinful secret was her husband's infidelity. What was his name? I can't even remember his name. She would never let his name be said out loud. She threw him out for sleeping with another woman. Kicked him out. Just like that. Judith divorced Leon, too. He kissed his mistress in his and Judith's very bedroom. I caught them accidentally. He laughed at me! "Why don't you go out and have some pleasure in life? Why are you always so faithful to that loser?" Imagine saying that about your own brother? I'd been to a doctor. The doctor examined me and told me I wasn't pregnant. Richard—where was Richard? Well, he wasn't there and I'd gone to spend the night with Mother Sybil. She terrified me, too. She was a mean, unloving, self-centered... bitch. Grandma Sybil only had one bed. I had to sleep with her. Oh, her smells! Her old-lady unguents and liniments. Don't open the window. I feel a draft. I feel a draft. She started talking to me in the dark. Telling me how much she'd loved him. Her husband. When they first came to America they scrubbed floors together. They'd meet in the middle and kiss. I don't know why but I thought that was very romantic. Then one day someone told her he was cavorting with a woman in Atlantic City. She didn't even let him pack. Her heart was still broken, she said, and she fell asleep crying. I kept waking up. I had to go to the toilet. I tiptoed in the dark. I didn't even flush. I was terrified I'd disturb her. The third or fourth time I smelled a bad smell. Like something spoiled or rotten. The fifth time I turned on the light. The toilet bowl was filled with blood. And lumps of stringy fibers. Like liver. Pieces of raw liver. From the butcher. I was so sleepy. The doctor had given me something to sleep. Why was liver coming out of me? And this awful smell? I went back to her bed. I had to go to the toilet again. And again. By morning I must have been close to death. She demanded her tea in bed. I pulled myself to the kitchen. I fell on the floor in a heap. What must have saved me was the kettle whistling. I couldn't reach up to turn it off. Where's my tea? What's wrong with you, girl? You can't even make my tea. I woke up in a hospital. I'd had a miscarriage. So you see how much I wanted you. Can't you? Can't you see how much I want you? (*Clutching* ALEXANDER *physically.*)

ALEXANDER: Momma, don't. I'm beginning to feel really unhappy.

RENA: Can't you see?

ALEXANDER: (*Breaking away from her.*) It comes out of nowhere.

NED: I get scared.

RENA: Can't you see?

(ALEXANDER *runs away from her.* RENA *has no arms to go to but* NED'*s; he accepts her reluctantly.*)

NED: Don't cry, Momma. (*In* ALEXANDER's *direction.*) Come back!

RENA: (*Clutching* NED.) You're leaving me. What am I supposed to do?

(BENJAMIN *enters; he doesn't like what he sees.* RENA *quickly relinquishes* NED.)

BENJAMIN: Hi, Mom.

RENA: I made your favorites. Remember when you were captain of the football team and drank three quarts of milk every meal?

BENJAMIN: I'm not on any team anymore. (*To* ALEXANDER.) Lemon, come help me.

(BENJAMIN *and* ALEXANDER *go off.* NED *returns to bed; he's not feeling well. Several yellow lights go on. The soft bell rings. He presses his buzzer.*)

RENA: (*Alone.*) Aren't you glad to see me?

(RENA *sits on the swing. After a moment,* RICHARD *enters.*)

RENA: Your other son has arrived.

RICHARD: I hate using everyone's toilet.

RENA: Year after year, you're the one who insists on coming back here to Mrs. Pennington's. We could go to that place in New Hampshire Manny and Teresa rave about. You even told me to send for a brochure. I've never been to Europe.

RICHARD: I've been to Europe. Leon and I tried to find where Pop was born. We couldn't find it. I like it here. Except for the toilet. (*Angry.*) We can't afford Europe, for Christ's sake!

RENA: I can dream! Let's have a nice time.

RICHARD: I didn't come here not to have a nice time. Why couldn't he have turned out like Ben?

RENA: You want another Ben? A son who never comes home. Who never writes except when he wants something. This is the first time the family has been together in years. I should've bought flowers. I wonder why he's come.

RICHARD: Come here.

RENA: What do you want?

RICHARD: (*As she sits beside him.*) You're a good egg. It hasn't been easy for you.

RENA: Why are you talking like this all of a sudden?

RICHARD: I'm just trying to be nice.

RENA: I don't even recognize it anymore.

RICHARD: You wanted more.

RENA: Everybody wants more.

RICHARD: I've always been crazy about you.

RENA: What's wrong with wanting more?

(NED *presses the buzzer more urgently.*)

RICHARD: Things will be better soon. Four more years and we'll have nothing to spend money on but ourselves.

RENA: Just the two of us again.

RICHARD: It will be better. We'll move back here for good.

RENA: You've never stopped loving me for one minute, have you?

RICHARD: No, Mommy, I haven't. And I never shall.

RENA: Richard, they're both gone now. I want to go out on my own now, too.

RICHARD: Don't start those dumb, stupid, asinine threats one more time!

(BENJAMIN *and* ALEXANDER *enter, carrying a tennis racket, books, a suitcase.*)

BENJAMIN: You could show a little more enthusiasm.

ALEXANDER: (*Offering his hand.*) Congratulations, Benjamin. I hope you'll be very happy.

(*But* BENJAMIN's *hands are full.*)

RICHARD: Hey, son!

BENJAMIN: Who won?

RICHARD: We slaughtered you. Yankees ten, Red Sox two.

BENJAMIN: We're still ahead in the series.

(HANNIMAN *runs in.*)

NED: I'm boiling! I feel like I'm going to explode!

(*She feels him, then quickly checks the monitoring devices.*)

RENA: (*Trying to kiss* BENJAMIN *hello.*) Tell me all about Yale. I want to know everything so I can be proud. What's your thesis on?

BENJAMIN: Ma, I've told you a dozen times.

RENA: Tell me again.

ALEXANDER: Twentieth Century Negro Poets.

(HANNIMAN *leaves quickly.*)

RENA: Isn't that fascinating.

RICHARD: Studying all that literature stuff is crap!

RENA: Don't be such a philistine!

BENJAMIN: It's my money and my education and my life.

(HANNIMAN *returns with* DR. DELLA VIDA. NED *begins to convulse slightly.*)

TONY: (*Checking the computer, then* NED.) He's going into shock! (*Turns off the machinery.*)

(HANNIMAN *hands him a huge syringe, which he injects into* NED's *groin or neck.*)

ALEXANDER: Benjamin doesn't want to go to law school. He wants to be a teacher or a writer. He wants to help people. Ned, what are they doing to you?

BENJAMIN: I'll be all right, Lemon. Law is helping people, too.

ALEXANDER: That's not what you told me! Ned, what's wrong? Why aren't you answering?

RICHARD: (*To* BENJAMIN.) Listen, mister smart ass big guy, don't make it sound like such a holy sacrifice! I got you this far. I got both of you this far. I got all of us this far.

RENA: Stop it, stop it, stop it!

ALEXANDER: *NED!*

RICHARD: You and your ungrateful prick of a brother!

RENA: We are not going to fight!

ALEXANDER: Why do you bring us back to this stupid place every year anyway? Just so we can feel poor? Benjamin is going to marry a rich girl he doesn't even love!

RENA: You're getting married?

RICHARD: Hey, I always say it's just as easy to marry a rich one.

BENJAMIN: You promised me you'd keep your mouth shut. Let's go for a swim. (*Throws* ALEXANDER *his suit.*)

RENA: Don't go. It's getting dark.

BENJAMIN: (*Gets his own suit.*) Fast!

RENA: It's too dark. Wait until tomorrow. I'll go with you.

RICHARD: (*Grabbing* ALEXANDER *as he starts out.*) Every time I look at you, every single time I see you, I wish to Christ your mother'd had that abortion!

RENA: (*A wail.*) NOOOOOO!

RICHARD: She wouldn't have another one. And I've been paying for it ever since.

RENA: I beg you!

ALEXANDER: Ned, help me! Where are you?

(NED *tries to get up, but is restrained by* DR. DELLA VIDA.)

(BENJAMIN *physically lifts* ALEXANDER *away from* RICHARD *and they start out.* RICHARD *grabs* RENA, *who is also leaving.*)

I'm going to be sick. (*Runs to sink.*)

TONY: It's okay, Ned. We're going to get through this.

RICHARD: Where do you think you're going? We can't afford another child, Rene. He'll just take all our pleasure away. All our money and all our hope.

RENA: Let go of me, Richard.

RICHARD: Listen to me, Rene. It's the Depression.

RENA: This time I mean it. This time I'm going for good.

(RICHARD *restrains her from leaving.*)

I only came back because you begged me! What else could I do? A woman can't get a decent job to use her brain. I had to sell lace and pins at Macy's for twelve dollars a week. I lost my chance with Drew Keenlymore.

RICHARD: We're back to him again? Miss Flirt! Miss God-damn Flirt!

BENJAMIN: (*Helping* ALEXANDER *at the sink.*) Lemon, are you all right?

ALEXANDER: Please don't call me Lemon anymore.

RICHARD: What does anyone know about not taking it anymore? Spending each day of my life at a job I hate, with people who don't know how smart I am.

BENJAMIN: Come on.

ALEXANDER: I can't throw up.

RICHARD: Not seeing my sons turn into anything I want as my sons—the one I love never at home, the other one always at home, to remind me of what a sissy's come out of my loving you. Don't leave me, Rene!

RENA: I am, I am. Let me go!

(RICHARD *is trying to hold a woman who doesn't want to be held. He hits her. She screams.*)

RICHARD: I don't want to live without you!

RENA: I'm supposed to stay here? For the rest of my life?

(RENA *breaks loose and runs off.* BENJAMIN *runs after her.* RICHARD *yanks* ALEXANDER *away from the sink and hurls him to the floor, falling on top of him, pinioning him beneath him and letting out all his venom and fury on his younger son.*)

RICHARD: You were a mistake! I didn't want you! I never wanted you! I should have shot my load in the toilet!

ALEXANDER: Mommy!

NED: (*Screaming out.*) Ben!

(BENJAMIN *runs back in. He somehow separates his father from his brother. He carries* ALEXANDER *off in his arms.*)

BENJAMIN: It's too late. There's nothing we can do. I shouldn't have come.

(RICHARD *pulls himself up off the floor. He doesn't know which way to go. He stumbles first in one direction, then in another, finally going off.*)

NED: It's too late. There's nothing we can do. I shouldn't have come.

HANNIMAN: Why we're just starting.

TONY: You just had a little imbalance. It's a good sign. It means we're knocking out more of your infected cells than we expected. I think we just may be seeing some progress.

NED: That was awful. You sure it's not just poison? Would you tell me it's working, even when it's killing me? Did anyone anywhere in the entire history of the world have a happy childhood?

TONY:　I'm sure George Bush was a very happy child.

HANNIMAN and NED:　He still is.

(*They all smile.* TONY *turns the switch to the equipment on again and leaves.* HANNIMAN *wipes* NED's *damp brow.*)

NED:　In eighteenth-century Holland—a country and culture that had never acted this way—there was a hysterical uprising against gays that resulted in the most awful witch hunts. Young boys were condemned, persecuted, throttled, executed... a fourteen-year-old boy was found guilty and drowned with a two hundred pound weight. Who was that kid? What was his name? What could he possibly ever have done to deserve such punishment, and in a Christian land?

　　Centuries later, historians, searching for a reason, discovered that, when all that happened, the sea walls along the Dutch coast were collapsing because of massive, unrelenting pressure from floods, accompanied by a plague of very hungry pile worms consuming the foundations.

　　The people, in that perverse cause-and-effect way that never seems to stop, had blamed the destruction of their coastline and its fortifications on the gay kids. God would inundate their Republic until it was punished and penance was paid to relieve the wrath of the Almighty.

　　When I was a little boy I thought colored girls were much sexier than white girls.

HANNIMAN:　What happened?

NED:　Boys. Any color. How did you meet Tony?

HANNIMAN:　I was head nurse of this division when he was appointed director.

NED: Was it love at first sight?

HANNIMAN: None of your business.

NED: You don't seem very happy. Is it because he's such a... Republican?

HANNIMAN: You think anyone black has anything to be happy about?

NED: It seems more personal.

HANNIMAN: Everyone in this entire hospital in every room on every floor is dying from something. They all come here to be saved. This is the new Lourdes. Congress gives us nine billion dollars a year to perform miracles. And God's a bit slow these days in the miracle department. You don't think that's enough to get you down?

NED: Still not personal enough.

HANNIMAN: You always say just what you want to?

NED: Pretty much. No matter what you say, x number of people are going to approve and x number aren't. You might as well say what you want to.

HANNIMAN: You obviously don't work for the government.

NED: So marrying a white man didn't solve any of your problems?

HANNIMAN: Did not marrying a colored girl solve any of yours? (*Starts to leave.*)

NED: Hey! I thought we were seeing some progress!

HANNIMAN: We are. (*Leaves.*)

ALEXANDER: (*Entering his Yale room, dressed most collegiately.*) The first thing upon entering a new life is to change one's name.

BEN: (*Entering with brownies and milk, wearing a Y athletic sweater.*) Ned?

ALEXANDER: Ben?

BEN: But Ben is logically the nickname for Benjamin.

ALEXANDER: I read this play called *Holiday* where there's a Ned. It could be a nickname for Alexander. It sounds very fresh and spiffy, don't you think? Ned. She still makes a good brownie.

BEN: (*Noticing some papers.*) What kind of dreadful way is this to start out? What happened?

ALEXANDER: What happened? I'm flunking psychology. And astronomy. And geology. And German. So far. What do I do?

BEN: Study.

ALEXANDER: That's very helpful. What did you win that letter for?

BEN: This one? Boxing, I think.

ALEXANDER: Boxing. Football. Squash. Tennis. Dean's List. Phi Bete. A after A after A. Prom committees, elected offices, scholarships, friends, girls . . . You have done your parents and your alma mater and your country proud. You're even marrying a rich girl.

BEN: It's time to get married.

ALEXANDER: Do you love her yet?

BEN: She's as good as anyone.

ALEXANDER: What kind of dreadful way is this to start out? I don't want to be a lawyer.

BEN: Nobody's asked you to be a lawyer.

ALEXANDER: I always dreamed we'd be partners in something.

BEN: Why aren't you going to Europe with Theo?

ALEXANDER: Boy, is *Moby Dick* a bitch to get excited about. Are you sorry Pop made you go to law school?

BEN: I don't believe anybody makes you do anything you don't really want to.

ALEXANDER: That's good to know.

BEN: Why aren't you going to Europe this summer with Theo all expenses paid? It sounded like a wonderful offer.

(NED *has left his bed and moved closer to* ALEXANDER.)

NED: This is one of those moments in life we talked about. Would life be otherwise if you did or didn't do something differently? You're about to tell your brother... something both painful and precious, something you don't understand, something you need help with. You want him to understand. Oh, how you want him to understand! He's not going to understand.

ALEXANDER: Will it be better if I don't tell him?

NED: I've always thought it would have been. I don't know. Why do you have to tell him at all?

ALEXANDER: Why not? Is it something so awful?

NED: (*Helplessly.*) But Ben is going to...

ALEXANDER:　Going to what?

NED:　(*Feebly.*) Make you...

ALEXANDER:　Make me what?

NED:　Make you do something I'd rather not have done. Just yet. They didn't know enough then!

ALEXANDER:　How much do they know now! In my limited experience, so far as I can see, you don't have a very good record on just about anything concerning me. Or yourself. Why are you even here? Why are you letting them do all this to you? Do you trust that doctor? I don't. He's much too gorgeous. (*To* BEN.) We were lovers.

BEN:　We were what!

ALEXANDER:　Me and Theo!

NED:　And so the journey begins. Do you feel any better?

BEN:　Did he ask you?

ALEXANDER:　(*To* BEN.) Yes. (*To* NED.) Yes!

BEN:　He shouldn't have done that.

ALEXANDER:　Oh, I wanted to do it.

BEN:　How can you be so certain of that?

ALEXANDER:　I don't believe anybody makes you do anything you don't really want to.

BEN:　This is about you, not me. Sometimes we do things we don't want to.

ALEXANDER:　Like become a lawyer and get married to someone you don't love?

BEN: Look, Sara and I are just getting started, and, listen, get off my case. What happened with Theo?

ALEXANDER: We made love. Right here. I went to Theo and asked him: I'm flunking out of your German class, could I do something for extra credit, and we went out and drank beer, and we came back here, and he asked me: would you like to make love, and I walked to this door, and opened it, and said: I think you'd better go, and I closed the door, and ran right back into his arms. And I passed.

BEN: I believe this is something they now think they can change.

ALEXANDER: It felt wonderful!

BEN: It's unhealthy, it's caused by something unhealthy, it'll do nothing but make you unhappy.

NED: How are all the men in my family such experts in these matters?

BEN: Everybody knows.

NED: Everybody does not know! Everybody is told!

BEN: What's the difference?

ALEXANDER: Unhealthy? (BEN *nods*.) Caused by something?

BEN: A possessive mother. An absent father.

NED: That's what they thought then.

ALEXANDER: Absent? Richard was always there. That was the problem. Possessive doesn't sound precise enough for Rena. (*To* NED.) Where do I get more up-to-date information?

BEN: You see a psychiatrist.

ALEXANDER: See him do what?

BEN: You talk to him.

ALEXANDER: Talk to *him?*

BEN: About this.

ALEXANDER: I'm talking to you.

BEN: What do you expect me to say?

ALEXANDER: "I don't care if you've got purple spots, I love you." Theo said there are lots of us. We can tell each other like Jewish people can.

BEN: Horseshit!

ALEXANDER: *We* mustn't fight, Benjamin.

NED: Why not? If you don't agree, fight, Alexander. Fight back! Never run away from a fight.

ALEXANDER: Which one of you am I supposed to fight? It's like Richard and Rena—each one is pulling so hard in opposite directions I'm being torn in two. (*To* NED.) Please call me Ned. (*To* BEN.) So you do think I'm sick? (*No answer.*) You do. I told Theo that going to Europe as his assistant on his Guggenheim was a terrific opportunity but that after walking round and around the block all night long I decided not to go.

BEN: Good man.

ALEXANDER: I told him no because I don't love him.

BEN: You told him no because you know it's wrong.

NED: (*To* BEN.) I told him no because... because I knew you wanted me to tell him no.

BEN: (*To* NED.) You told him no because you knew it was considered wrong and unhealthy and sick.

ALEXANDER: Don't I just not love Theo because I just don't love Theo?

BEN: There's something called psychoanalysis. It's the latest thing. You lie down on a couch every day and say whatever comes into your head.

NED: (*As* ALEXANDER *looks at him, suddenly worried.*) Why listen to me? I can only predict epidemics and plagues.

ALEXANDER: What have I done?

NED: You're letting Ben push you on to a treadmill of revolving doctors, not one of whom will know a fucking thing about what makes *your* heart tick.

ALEXANDER: What will they do to me?

NED: They will turn you into a productive human being.

ALEXANDER: What's wrong with that? I'm flunking every course.

NED: While they teach you to love yourself they will also teach you to hate your heart. It's their one great trick. All these old Jewish doctors—the sons of Sigmund—exiled from their homelands, running from Hitler's death camps, for some queer reason celebrated their freedom on our shores by deciding to eliminate homosexuals. That's what you are. It's going to be a long time before you can say the word out loud. Over and over and over again they will pound into your consciousness through constant repetition: you're sick, you're sick, you're sick. So your heart is going to lie alone. So you see, you should have gone to Europe with Theo.

ALEXANDER: Ben—I'm scared.

BEN: You're making all the right decisions. I'll always fight for you and defend you and protect you. All I ask is that you try. The talking cure, it's called. (*Puts his arm around* ALEXANDER's *shoulder*.)

ALEXANDER: Talking? I should be cured real fast. (*Leaving with* BEN.) Theo gave me crabs. Do you know what crabs are? (BEN *nods*.) I didn't but I do now.

(*They exit.* HANNIMAN *enters with her cart. Sounds of chanting outside can be dimly heard.*)

HANNIMAN: We need more blood.

NED: What are you opening, a store? Do you know how many blood tests I've had in the past twelve years? It's definitely a growth industry. The tyranny of the blood test. Ladies and gentlemen, step right up and watch the truth drawn right before your very eyes. We are being tested for the presence of a virus that may or may not be the killer. We are being tested to discover if this and/or that miraculous new discovery that may or may not kill the virus which may or may not be the killer is working. We live in constant terror that the number of healthy cells, which may or may not be an accurate indicator of anything at all and which the virus that may or may not be the killer may or may not be destroying, will decline and fall. What does any of this *mean*? Before each blood test, no one sleeps. (*Singing*.) "Nessun dorma." Awaiting each result, the same. The final moments are agony. On a piece of paper crowded with computerized chitchat that, depending on whom you ask, is open to at least two and often more contradictory interpretations, and which your doctor is holding in his hand, is printed the latest clairvoyance of your life expectancy. May I have the winning envelope, please?

HANNIMAN: Boy, you are one piece of cake. What happened between you and your people out there?

NED: You ran out of miracles.

HANNIMAN: Not personal enough.

NED: They look to me for leadership and I don't know how to guide them. I'm going to die and they're going to die, only they're nineteen and twenty-four and somehow born into this world and I feel so fucking guilty that I've failed them. I wanted to be Moses but I only could be Cassandra.

HANNIMAN: And you lay all that on yourself?

NED: Why not?

HANNIMAN: If people don't want to be led, they don't want to be led. You're not as grand and important as you think you are.

NED: In a few more years more Africans will be dying from this plague than are being born. If this stuff works, only rich white men will get it. I call that genocide. What do you call it? How do you go to sleep at night lying beside your husband knowing all that? What are you doing for *your* people out there?

HANNIMAN: I don't have to take this shit. (*Walks out.*)

NED: (*Calling after her.*) You're as grand and important as you want to be!

(*Loud banging is heard, then* BEN's *voice.*)

BEN: Ned! Your landlady says you're in there! Open up. Open up the goddamned door! Alexander!

(BEN *is banging on the door of a sparsely furnished New York studio apartment.* ALEXANDER *sits staring into space.* BEN *finally breaks the door down. He carries a bottle of champagne.*)

You haven't been to work in a week. Your office said you were home sick. Why don't you answer the phone? Does Dr.... I can't remember the new one's name... know you're like this? Ned, come on, talk to me. You always talk to me. Ned, goddamn it, please answer me! You know, you're not a very good uncle. You never come and see my kids. Alexandra would like to see her namesake. Timmy wants to know all about the movie business. Betsy—sometimes I think my feelings for my firstborn are unnatural. Have you been staring into space for a week? Come on—congratulations! You're going to London! Your career is progressing nicely. Are you going to talk to me?

(BEN *uncorks the champagne.* NED *gives him a cup.* BEN *pours some and offers it to* ALEXANDER, *who refuses.*)

ALEXANDER: Be careful you don't ever give me one of your secrets.

NED: I told you not to tell him.

ALEXANDER: Fuck you! (*Mimicking:*) "I told you this!" "I told you that!" I've had enough of your... lack of cooperation.

NED: Well, tough shit and fuck you yourself, you little parasite.

ALEXANDER: Parasite?

NED: Bloodsucker. Leech. Hanger-on. Freeloader. You're like the very virus itself and I can't get rid of you.

ALEXANDER: I didn't know that's what you wanted to do.

NED: There's never been a virus that's been successfully eradicated.

ALEXANDER: (*Repeating.*) I didn't know that's what you wanted to do.

BEN: Who is it this time?

(BEN *offers him the cup of champagne again. This time* ALEXANDER *takes it.* BEN *drinks out of the bottle.*)

ALEXANDER: Six shrinks later I'm still the most talkative one in class. When do I graduate? You always take care of me. Why? (*No answer.*) Why?

BEN: Tell me about him.

ALEXANDER: Which one?

BEN: Any one.

ALEXANDER: Dr. Schwartz kept calling me a pervert. Dr. Grossman said I was violating God's laws by not fathering children. Dr. Nussbaum was also very uncomplimentary. I ran into him getting fucked in the Provincetown dunes. Dr.... I go to all the doctors you send me to. One doesn't do the trick, you find me another.

BEN: What's wrong!

ALEXANDER: I didn't know life could be so lonely.

BEN: I'm sorry. You'll meet someone.

ALEXANDER: Oh, that. I already tried that. Hundreds of times. At first I wanted love back. But now I'm willing to give that up if someone would just stay put and let me love him. That's really a person who likes himself a lot, huh?

BEN: Don't give up. Your self-pity will... diminish.

ALEXANDER: I did meet someone. He loved every book I loved. Every symphony and pop song and junk food. I couldn't believe this man was interested in me. He was so... beautiful. Beauty rarely looks at me. I couldn't stop feeling his skin, touching his face. (*Pointing to mattress.*) Right there. There! All night long, two days through, we couldn't let go of each other.

And then came the brainwashing session. What did that mind-bender say to turn me into such a monster? I walked home very slowly. I came in here. Peter had made breakfast. Nobody ever made me breakfast. He smiled and said, "I've missed you." He missed me. "We have one more day before I have to go back." He was finishing his doctorate at Harvard. The perfect man for *anyone* to take home to the folks. And I said... I actually said... I don't know where the words came from or how I could say them... but I said: "You have to leave now." God damn you!

BEN: Me?

ALEXANDER: They're your witch doctors! (*To* NED.) All this psychoanalysis shit and you're what I've got to show for it?

NED: I did not send you into psychoanalysis.

ALEXANDER: Stop trying to keep your hands so fucking clean! *You're* the bloodsucker!

BEN: Ned... ?

ALEXANDER: Why do I go to them? One after another. One doesn't do the trick: step right up, your turn at bat. Why do I listen to them? Why do I listen to you? How do we still love each other, when all we do is... this? Peter could be here (*Holding out his empty arms.*) right now. Why are you so insistent? Why do I obey you? You don't put a gun to my head. Why don't I say: get out of my life, I'll make my own rules? I could be loved! But you do put a gun to my head. You won't love me unless I change. Well, it's too powerful a force to change! It's got to be a part of me! It doesn't want to die. And fights tenaciously to stay alive, against all odds. And no matter what anyone does to try and kill it. Why don't you just leave me alone? We don't have to see each other. Are you afraid to let go of me, too? Why? Why am I—why are we both—such collaborators? And how can I love you when part of me thinks you're murdering me?

BEN: You're very strange. You just lay it all right out there. You always have.

NED: (*To* BEN.) Answer him!

BEN: What do you want me to say! (*Pause.*) Change is hard.

ALEXANDER: How about grief? And sadness. And mourning for lost life and love and what might have been.

BEN: Try not to be so melodramatic.

ALEXANDER: Melodramatic? Who are you? Do I know you? Sometimes you can be a very mysterious person.

BEN: I've heard excellent things about another doctor. In London.

ALEXANDER: Why'd you stay away from home so much? (*No answer.*) Why'd you stay away from home? (*No answer.*) Why did you run away?

BEN: I didn't run away.

ALEXANDER: You were never there.

NED: Answer him!

BEN: (*After a long pause.*) I didn't have a mother.

ALEXANDER: You never had a *mother?*

BEN: You asked me why I never came home. That's why I never came home.

ALEXANDER: You thought Rena didn't love you?

BEN: She doesn't.

ALEXANDER: Mommy doesn't love you? (*To* NED.) Did you know this?

NED: That's what he believes.

BEN: She was never there! She had so many jobs. She was always out taking care of everyone in the entire world except me. So I went out and did a thousand projects at a time because I thought that was how I'd get my mother's love. If I got *another* A or headed up *another* organization, she'd notice me and pay attention to me and I'd win some approval from her. I needed her and she wasn't there and I resent it bitterly. (*Long pause.*) And I'll never forgive her for that.

ALEXANDER: (*Shaken, feeling he must defend her.*) She had to work! Pop didn't make enough! She was doing her best.

BEN: That's all she cares about. *Her* best. She *made* Daddy quit working for Uncle Leon. It was a good job. All through the Depression, Leon was rich. Pop had been making big bucks. Suddenly he's no longer the breadwinner, with no self-respect. He was out of work for something like seven, eight years before the war finally came and there was work in Washington for everybody. So we moved to Washington where he made ten times less than he'd made with Leon.

ALEXANDER: You can't blame that on her!

BEN: Why not! She had to be the star. She never stopped. She had a million jobs. She had a few spare hours she ran over to take dictation from a couple of bozos who repaired wrecked trucks. Leon found Pop a job as American counsel in the Virgin Islands. A big house, servants, tax-free salary. A fortune in those days. They turned it down.

ALEXANDER: She said there wasn't any milk for babies. You were just born.

BEN: You boil milk. You use powdered. What did all the tens of thousands of babies born there drink? Have you heard about any mass demise of Virgin Island babies? She didn't want to go! She felt so "useful." And so he stayed home, unemployed, playing pinochle with the boys.

ALEXANDER: Why didn't he hustle his ass like she did?

BEN: You're not listening to me. She took his balls away! Why are you defending her so? She almost smothered you to death.

ALEXANDER: She was the only one interested in me!

BEN: Interested in you? What did she ever do to help you develop one single ability or interest or gift you ever had? You wanted to act, sing, dance, write, create... whatever. That's what parents are supposed to do! Richard crucified every single one of those desires and she stood by and let him. All she does is talk endlessly and forever about herself!

ALEXANDER: It wasn't her. It wasn't! It was him. It was all him. It was Richard. Why aren't you mad at him for being so weak instead of her for trying to be strong?

BEN: She called all the shots and she called them from her own selfish point of view.

ALEXANDER: You don't like her as much as I don't like him. What happens when a kid is chosen for the wrong team?

It's as if we each took one parent for our very own. And each of them chose one of us. The whole procedure had nothing to do with love. Can you say I love you? Out loud? To anyone? And mean it? (*No answer. To* NED.) Can you? (*No answer.*)

BEN: There's just an anger inside me that never goes away. I've got to get out of here. I'm late. Walk me back to the office.

ALEXANDER: How'd you figure all this out? (*No answer.*) You have just told me I shouldn't love my mother. How did you figure this all out!

BEN: (*Another long pause.*) I'm being psychoanalyzed.

ALEXANDER: (*Pause.*) I don't know why but that scares the shit out of me.

BEN: It should make you feel better you're not the only one.

ALEXANDER: It's all the decisions I let you make for me because you were the only one. What happened? God, wouldn't it be wonderful if it were another man.

BEN: You know how Richard always yelled at you, no matter what you did, you couldn't do anything right? That's how Sara treats Timmy. She says I... I withhold. I don't show how I feel toward anyone and that makes her overreact and overreach and vent her anger on young Timmy. My son... he... she... she's so hard on him, she takes everything out on him that's meant for me. I called her... a controlling bitch. She says she can't stop herself from doing it. Alexander, it's a mess. The poor kid's got some kind of stomach ulceration now. He'll suddenly start bleeding, he can never be out of range of a toilet, and he's only a kid, he'll have this all his life. He's such a good kid. He came into my

room and started crying. I want him to be smart in school
and the kid just isn't. And he knows it disappoints the shit
out of me. Ned, why doesn't he do better? He's smart. I
just know it! He was crying. He started screaming I didn't
love him. And I'd never loved him. Why are you looking
at me that way? We're working on it! Sara's in therapy,
too. She's learning. I'm learning. Richard and Rena couldn't
learn. We can learn. We mustn't stop trying to learn.

NED: "And the sins of the fathers shall visit unto the third
and fourth generations."

BEN: No! I don't believe that! We *can* change it!

NED: And all those years you told me it was worse for me
and I believed you!

BEN: It was. It was worse for you.

NED: No, it wasn't. Why was it so important for you to hold
on to that? Why was it so important to you to make me the
sick one? Were you so angry at Rena that you had to make
my homosexuality so awful just to blame her? It wasn't so
hot for either of us! It made you stay away from home.
And it didn't make me gay. It made both of us have a great
deal of difficulty saying "I love you."

BEN: Ned—go and call Peter back.

ALEXANDER: Thank you, Ben. I called Peter back. I asked
him to meet me. Which he did. At the Savoy Plaza. I took
this grand suite and ordered filet mignon and champagne
and flowers, tons of flowers. I apologized over and over
again for what I had done. He said he recalled our time
together as very pleasant. I practically pounced on him and
threw him on the bed and held him in my arms and kissed
him all over. He told me he was very happily in love with

someone else and he thought it best that he leave. Which he did.

BEN: I'm sorry. I have to get back to the office. I really am sorry. I have a meeting. Good luck in London. Maybe you'll meet someone.

ALEXANDER: Are you saying loving a man is now okay?

BEN: Keep fighting. Keep on fighting. Don't give up. The answers will present themselves. They really will. For both of us!

(*They go off.*)

NED: I haven't been honest with you. I left out the hardest part for me to talk about. It was done by another Ned, someone inside of me who took possession of me and did something I've been terrified, every day of my life ever since, he might come back and do again. And, this time, succeed. After my father beat me and Mom up and told me he'd never wanted me and after I told my brother I was gay and after my brother got married and before my first year's final exams that I knew I'd flunk, I pulled a bottle of some kind of pills which belonged to my roommate who's father was a doctor out of his bureau drawer and swallowed them all. I had wanted to take a knife and slice a foot or arm off. I had wanted to see blood, gushing everywhere, making a huge mess, and floating me away on its sea. But there were only pills. I'm only going to take two for a headache and two more to help me sleep. I have finals on Monday and there's no way I can pass. Where else can I go? Back to Eden Heights? I'd rather be dead. So where? Every social structure I'm supposed to be a part of—my family, my religion, my school, my friends, my neighbor-hood, my work, my city, my state, my country, my government, my newspaper, my television... —tells me over and over what I feel and see and think and do is sick. The only safe place left is the dark. I want to go to sleep. It's Friday. I want to sleep till Tuesday. (*Swallowing* HANNIMAN'*s pills with* BEN'*s champagne.*) This couple of pills will take me till tomorrow and these until Sunday and... Monday... now I can sleep till Tuesday. Might as well take a few more. Just in case. Pop's right, of course. I'm a failure. (*Looking at himself in the mirror over the sink.*) You even look like Richard. You'll look like him for the rest of your life. I am more my father's child than ever I wanted to be. I've fought so hard not to look like you. I've fought so hard not to inherit your failure. Poor newly-named Ned. Trying so hard to fight failure. Now increasing at an awful rate. I woke up in the hospital and Ben was there beside me.

ALEXANDER'S VOICE: Help! I'm drowning! Don't let me drown!

NED: That night at Mrs. Pennington's when Benjamin stopped Poppa from beating me up, he put me on his shoulders and carried me down to the shore. We swam and played and ducked under each other's arms and legs. We lay on the big raft, way out on the Sound, side by side, not saying a word, looking at the stars. I held his hand. He said, Come dive with me. I dived in after he did and I got caught under the raft and I couldn't get out from under. I thrashed desperately this way and that and I had no more breath.

ALEXANDER'S VOICE: Help! I'm drowning! Don't let me drown!

NED: When I thought I would surely die, he rescued me and saved me, Benjamin did.

(BENJAMIN *carries in a limp* ALEXANDER *and lays him on the ground. Both are wet from the ocean.*)

He got me to the shore and he laid me out on the sand and he pressed my stomach so the poison came out and he kissed me on the lips so I might breathe again.

TONY: (*Entering.*) Ned, I've run the tests. The new genes are adhering. We're half way there. We can go on with the final part. Say Thank You. Say Congratulations. You begged for a few more years. I may have bought you life. (*Leaves.*)

NED: Okay, Ned—be happy. Be exuberant! You're half way there. (*Singing.*) "Hold my hand and we're half way there, Hold my hand and I'll take you there. Someday. Somewhere. Somehow..."

End of Act Two

ACT THREE

(HANNIMAN *removes three more sacks of blood from the small insulated chest on her cart and inserts them into the wall machine.* DR. DELLA VIDA, *wearing the white dress uniform of a Public Health Service officer, checks that everything is in readiness.* NED, *wearing a navy blue robe with a red ribbon on the lapel, looks out the window.*)

NED: Three hundred and seventy arrests and not one lousy reporter or camera so no one sees it but a couple hundred of your scientists with nothing better to do than look out their windows because their microscopes are constipated.

TONY: I thought your soapbox was in retirement.

NED: You bought me life.

TONY: Nice robe.

NED: Navy blue and red. The smart colors Felix always called them.

(TONY *wheels in from the outside hallway a new machine—the Ex-Cell-Aerator, another elaborate invention, replete with its own dials and switches and tubings and lights.*)

What's that?

TONY: (*Proudly.*) I call it the Ex-Cell-Aerator. Your reassembled blood will be pumped through it so it can be exposed to particles of—

NED: That's it? I thought it was the other one.

TONY: It's both of them.

NED: It takes two? Did you dream all this up?

TONY: I try to be as creative as the law allows.

NED: (*Re: the sacks of blood.*) The little buggers went and multiplied.

TONY: Enriched. They got enriched. Hey, don't touch those.

NED: Do genes get loose and act uncontrollably, like viruses?

TONY: You bet. It's scary trying to modify nature.

NED: Despite everything I know and said and stood for, I have fucked with the enemy and he has given me hope.

TONY: I'm not your enemy.

NED: Why are you all dressed up?

TONY: The President wants to know all about this. (*Indicates that* NED *should get in bed.*)

NED: Any of my blood you want to slip him, hey... You're going to the White House!

TONY: Yes, I am. I go quite often.

NED: (*As* TONY *and* HANNIMAN *reconnect him to the wall tubing.*) Tell me... you're a doctor, but you're also an officer in the service of your country. You're compelled to obey orders. How can research be legislated? You're an artist. How can you be free enough to create? It's like asking writers to write not using any vowels.

TONY: (*Connecting the Ex-Cell-Aerator to the wall apparatus.*) I run the premier research facility in the entire world. The American people are very lucky to have a place like this. And you got him all wrong. He's a good guy. He's got a heart. He really wants this disease to go away.

NED: He's brain dead and you're brainwashed.

TONY: Lay off my wife, will you? Any fights you got with me, pick them with me. (*Hits a computer key to start everything going.*)

NED: Tony, all your top assistants are gay. What's that all about? When I bring down all my young men for meetings, you look at them so... (*Can't find the word.*)

TONY: So what?

NED: You can't take your eyes off them.

TONY: It's very sad... what's happening.

NED: Yes, it is. What kind of life do you want to be leading that you're not? Why is everyone down here afraid to call a plague a plague? Are you punishing us or yourself? (*Calling after him as he leaves.*) You get away with murder because you're real cute and everybody wants to go to bed with you! Nobody wanted to go to bed with Ed Koch. Him we could get rid of. (*Talking to the Ex-Cell-Aerator.*) *You're* the cure? I hope you come in a portable version, like a laptop. Can you find me a boy friend while you're at it? Way to win the charm contest, Ned. You'll never get them in your arms that way. Mom, you said there wasn't anything in the world your son couldn't do.

(HANNIMAN *comes in and pulls a curtain around the bed.*

RENA, *now about seventy, sits in a hospital waiting area trying unsuccessfully to read some old magazines. Occasionally she gets up to look inside a room through an open door.*

After a moment, NED, *wearing an overcoat and carrying a suitcase, enters. They are strangely distant with each other. Sounds of baseball game on the TV.*)

RENA: (*To the unseen* RICHARD.) I'm closing this so I don't have to hear that ball game. (*Does so.*) When he sees you here he'll put two and two together and realize we sent for you.

NED: Doesn't he know?

RENA: Some things you don't want to know, even if you know. How's London? You never write to me.

NED: It's great. Very productive. Where's Ben?

RENA: They took a break. Sara's been wonderful. She hasn't left my side. So.

NED: You always wanted to travel.

RENA: He isn't dead yet.

NED: I'm just saying you've got something to look forward to.

RENA: How about giving me a chance to mourn first? Why are we talking like this to each other? I haven't seen you in six, seven years. Are you still going to a psychiatrist?

NED: I can go every day for seventy-five dollars a week.

RENA: That used to be three months' rent. How in God's name do you find enough to talk about every day?

NED: I fall asleep a lot.

RENA: You pay someone to fall asleep? You kids, you and your psychiatrists think you know it all. Then why aren't we perfect after all these years?

NED: Did you and Richard have a good sex life?

RENA: That's none of your business.

NED: I just thought I'd ask.

RENA: Well, don't.

NED: Did he want sex more than you, or did you want it and he wouldn't?

RENA: Stop it!

NED: You used to tell me everything.

RENA: Well, here's something I'm not going to. Our lives weren't about sex. Is sex what controls your life?

NED: I don't know. Why don't you try and look up Drew Keenlymore?

RENA: Why don't you try and stop being so fresh?

NED: Didn't you love him?

RENA: Why are you so obsessed with Drew Keenlymore?

NED: One should be able to have the man one loves.

RENA: Life should be a lot of things.

NED: Did he ever ask you to marry him? Did he?

RENA: I was invited to the Keenlymore private island estate in Western Canada for the entire summer. What does that tell you?

NED: But you didn't go.

RENA: He was ready to marry me. There! Does that make you happy?

NED: If you'd listened to your heart, and not been so afraid, that would have made me happy.

RENA: Listen to my heart. You've seen too many movies. Have you listened to your heart? I don't hear about any secret long-lost love you're keeping in a purse on the top shelf of your closet.

NED: I don't fall in love. People don't fall in love with me.

RENA: That's too bad.

NED: I want to love them. I want them to love me back.

RENA: Everyone should have someone.

NED: Kids are some sort of sum total of both their parents. We pick up a lot of traits from whatever kind of emotional subtext is going on.

RENA: I'm supposed to understand that mouthful of jargon?

NED: We've got both of you in us.

RENA: Are we getting blamed for all of this?

NED: I've just finally got the courage to say what I want to say.

RENA: I don't recall your ever being delinquent in that department. Well, I always tried to instill courage in you. But you can't always just say what you think.

NED: You saw how much Pop hated me. You must have had some sense that if you'd only left him, I wouldn't have had to go through all that shit.

RENA: Don't use that language. I tried to make up for it by loving you more.

NED: It doesn't work that way.

RENA: It would appear it doesn't.

NED: Why didn't you leave him for good?

RENA: You don't run away when things don't work out.

NED: You ran away from Drew.

RENA: Some courage I had and some courage I didn't have. I don't cry over spilt milk.

NED: Are you admitting you didn't love your husband?

RENA: I am not! You don't have so many choices as you seem to think!

NED: I'm homosexual. I would like you to accept that but I don't care if you don't, because I have.

RENA: You don't care? So I was a lousy mother.

NED: Don't do that.

RENA: Why not? You just said I was. Not very good value for all my years, is it? Some psychiatrist, some stranger, turns your son against you and declares me a bad mother.

NED: The preference now is to stay away from judgmental words like good or bad.

RENA: Of course it's judgmental! Is this some kind of joke? You think any mother likes her son to be a... I'm not even going to say the word, that's how judgmental I think it is. I never criticized my parents. I worshiped the ground my mother walked on. I respected my father, even if he wasn't the most affectionate man in the world.

NED: Your father never smiled a day in his life.

RENA: Life was hard! They ran a tiny grocery store in a hostile neighborhood where neither of them spoke English and all the customers were Irish Catholics who hated us and never paid their bills. My parents didn't marry for love. They married to stay alive! Most kids grow up and leave home. You left home and found new parents called psychiatrists. I'm sorry the old ones were so disappointing. Sum total? Of both of us? You can also be so much more than that. I always told your father he should show his feelings more. He couldn't do it. He never would talk about his dreams. I don't even know what his dreams were. I guess they were taken away from him before I even knew him. He really did love you! I knew someday we'd reap the whirlwind. Why didn't Ben become one, too? He was there, too.

NED: I'm beginning to think it isn't caused by anything. I was born this way.

RENA: I don't believe that.

NED: I like being gay. It's taken me a very, very, very long time. I don't want to waste any more, tolerating your being ashamed of me, or anyone I care about being ashamed of me. If you can't accept that, you won't see your younger son again.

RENA: He has to die for you even to come home as it is. It makes you happy? Anything that makes you happy makes me happy. Miss Pollyanna, that's me. Go say hello to your father. Please don't tell him your wonderful news that makes you so happy.

(*She takes his suitcase from him and goes off.* NED *pulls the curtain around the bed, revealing* RICHARD *in it, half asleep, with the ball game still on.* NED *comes in and turns the TV off.* RICHARD *wakes up.*)

RICHARD: Who won?

NED: Hi, Pop.

RICHARD: This is it, boy. I'm not going to make it.

NED: Sure you are.

RICHARD: I'm ready to go.

NED: Hey, I want you to see my first movie. I wrote it and produced it. It's good!

RICHARD: My goddamned Yankees can't break their losing streak. Ben's goddamned Red Sox may win the pennant.

NED: It cost two million dollars. I was paid a quarter of a million dollars.

RICHARD: Movies. The thee-ay-ter. When are you going to grow up?

NED: I've discovered how to make a living from it.

RICHARD: At least Ben listened to me. He's raking it in. He's senior partner over two hundred lawyers. Two million dollars. That's a hot one. I'm glad it's over. What's your name now?

NED: I've been Ned since I was eighteen.

RICHARD: Eighteen. That's when your mother started signing over her paychecks to your psychiatrist. I wouldn't have anything to do with it. She could have bought lots of nice clothes. She could have looked real pretty. I never felt good. I've felt sick all my life. In and out of doctors' offices and still the pain in my bloody gut. Nothing ever took it away.

I never had a father either. So long, boy. (*He rolls over, with his back to* NED.)

NED: What do you mean, you never had a father either? (*No answer.*) Pop? Poppa? (RICHARD *doesn't answer.* NED *starts out...*)

RICHARD: My father was a mohel. You know what that is?

NED: The man who does the circumcision.

RICHARD: It was supposed to be a holy honor. God was supposed to bless him and his issue forever. One day he cut too much foreskin and this rich baby was mutilated for life. My Mom and Pop ran away and changed our name. Then Pop ran away. Forever.

NED: Mom said Grandma Sybil threw him out for sleeping with another woman in Atlantic City.

RICHARD: That's what she told people. He ran away when the kid he mutilated grew up and tracked him down. He couldn't have an erection without great pain and he was out for Pop's blood. I never told anyone. Not even your mother. I was afraid if I told her she wouldn't marry me. Maybe I should have told her. I wanted her more than she wanted me. I thought I could convince her and I never could. I helped my father. I was his assistant. All the time, the blood. Bawling babies terrified out of their wits. Tiny little cocks with pieces peeled off them. I had to dispose of the pieces. I buried them. He made me memorize all the Orthodox laws. If I made a mistake, he beat me. "You are forbidden to touch your membrum in self-gratification. You are forbidden to bring on an erection. It is forbidden to discharge semen in vain. Two bachelors must not sleep together. Two bachelors must not gaze upon each other. Two bachelors who lie down together and know each other and touch each other, it is equal to killing a person and saying blood is all over my hands. It is forbidden... It is forbidden..." He made me learn all that and then he ran away. I never stopped hating him. It's hard living with your gut filled with hate. Good luck to you, boy. Anything you want to say to me?

(RICHARD *rolls over and turns his back on him.* NED *stands there, trying to work up his courage to say what he has to say. Finally, finally, he does so.*)

NED: I'm sorry your life was a disappointment, Poppa. Poppa, you were cruel to me, Poppa.

(*There is no answer. He pulls the curtain closed again.*)

Poppa died. I didn't cry. My movie was a success. I made another. I realized how little pleasure achievement gave me. Slowly I became a writer. It suited me. I'd finally found a way to make myself heard. And "useful"—that word Rena so reveled in trumpeting. I would address the problems of my new world. Every gay man I knew was fucking himself to death. I wrote about that. Every gay man I knew wanted a lover. I wrote about that. I said that having so much sex made finding love impossible. I made my new world very angry. As when I was a child, such defiance made me flourish. My writing and my notoriety prospered.

I stopped going to psychoanalysts. I'd analyzed, observed, regurgitated, parsed, declined, X-rayed, and stared down every action, memory, dream, recollection, thought, instinct, and deed, from every angle I'd been able to come up with.

(NED *pulls back the curtain and gets into bed. He reconnects himself to the tubing.*)

I spent many years looking for love—in the very manner I'd criticized. How needy man is. And with good reason. When I finally met someone, I was middle-aged. His name was Felix Turner. Eleven months later he was sick and nineteen months later he was dead. I had spent so many years looking for and preparing for and waiting for Felix. Just as he came into my arms and just as I was about to say "I love you, Felix," the plague came along and killed him. And the further away I've got from the love I had, the more I question I ever had it in the first place.

Ben invested my money wisely and I am rich. When I get angry with him for not joining me in fighting this plague, he points out that he has made me financially independent so I could afford to be an activist. Ben has made all the Weeks family, including Rena and his children, rich. That's what he wanted to do—indeed I believe that's been his mission in life—to give all of us what he and I never had as children—and he's accomplished it.

(BEN *stands in the Eden Heights apartment, smoking a cigar. Scattered cartons and packing crates.*)

NED: Did you ever think you'd spend one more night in Eden Heights?

BEN: I consider it one of the greatest achievements of my life that I got out of here alive.

NED: Don't you ever stop and think how far we've come?

BEN: No. Never.

(RENA *is on the phone. She is now almost ninety.* BEN *sits in a chair and reads a business magazine.*)

RENA: (*Loudly.*) I'm coming home! I'll be there tomorrow! Back with all you dear chums I've loved since childhood! I can hardly wait! (*Hangs up.*) The woman's deaf. Paula's deaf and Nettie's moved to an old people's kibbutz in Israel and Belle is blind and Lydia's dead. Belle's husband brought you both into this world. Lydia introduced me to Richard. She didn't want him. (*Starts rummaging in a carton.*) All our past—in one battered carton from the Safeway. Aah, I'm going to throw it all away.

NED: No, I want it. It's our history.

RENA: Some history. So you can dredge up more unhappy memories to tell a psychiatrist how much you hated your father.

NED: (*To* BEN.) Don't you want to take anything for a memento?

BEN: You're the family historian. I leave the past to you.

NED: Your West Point letters, your yearbooks...

BEN: I've burned the mortgage. You're the one with the passion for remembering.

NED: Is that the way we handle it? I remember and you don't?

BEN: Maybe so. Maybe you've hit the nail on the head, young brother.

RENA: (*Comes across* RICHARD's *watch chain.*) He was Phi Beta Kappa and Law Journal. He majored in Greek and Latin. They didn't let many Jews into Yale in those days. You would have thought he'd have done better.

NED: Both brothers such failures. Uncle Leon wound up broke, hanging around the Yale Club trying to bum loans off old Yalies.   could never understand why you paid for his funeral.

BEN: He wasn't such a bad guy.

RENA: Aunt Judith threw him out when she discovered all his bimbos.

BEN: Some old judge I met told me, "If only Leon had been castrated instead of circumcised, he'd have wound up on the Supreme Court."

RENA: I've lived in this room for over fifty years. We moved down here on a three-month temporary job. Some man had almost burned to death and they needed a new one fast. The poor chap died and the job was Richard's. (*Comes across the navy blue crocheted purse and pulls out the letters and tries to read them.*)

NED: Ah, the famous letters. (*Knows them by heart.*) "I find my schedule will perhaps bring me into the vicinity of New York on 4th May; might you be available for luncheon?"

RENA: That was at Delmonico's.

NED: "I find I must reschedule; will you be available instead on the 10th inst.?" "It now appears the 10th must be re-placed by the 20th and even this is not firm." Why did I think they were so romantic?

RENA: They were romantic. They are romantic.

NED: Maybe you'll meet another man at the home.

RENA: It's called an adult residence. I don't want to meet another man. One was enough. I always thought Richard was inadequate. I just never had the guts to really leave him. It's no great crime to choose security over passion. My grand passion was the two of you. (*To* BEN.) You have the wonderful wife and the wonderful marriage and have given me my wonderful grandchildren. (*To* NED.) You have the artistic talent, which you inherited from me. Hurry up and write whatever it is you're going to write about me so I can get through all the pain it'll no doubt cause me.

NED: Why do you automatically assume it will be painful?

RENA: Knowing you it will be. I want to show you something. (*Goes into her bedroom.*)

BEN: We can't die. We're indestructible. We have her genes inside us. Sara called. Timmy has to have an operation. But then it should be fine. His bleeding will stop. Finally. All these years we blamed ourselves. It wasn't bad parenting. It wasn't psychosomatic. It was genetic. Ulcerated nerve ends not dissimilar to what Richard must have had.

NED: I'm glad. Genetic. That's what they say now about homosexuality. In a few more minutes the Religious Right is going to turn violently Pro-Choice.

BEN: Now if Betsy wouldn't keep falling for all these wretched young men who treat her so terribly.

NED: Yes, that's a tough one.

BEN: But I've found her the best therapist I could find.

NED: Her very own first therapist.

BEN: We learned how to attack problems and not be defeated by them. We found the tools to do this, probably by luck and the accident of history. Rena and Richard didn't. For them it was more about missed opportunities. It was the wrong time for them and it hasn't been for us.

NED: For you.

BEN: Ned, you're not going to die. Tell Rena I'll be here with the car in the morning at nine sharp.

(RENA *comes back dressed in the Russian peasant clothing.*)

NED: How *did* we get out of here alive?

BEN: A lot of expensive therapy. (*Sneaks out.*)

RENA: I wore this when I got off the boat from Russia.

NED: You were two years old when you got off the boat from Russia. (*Pause.*) I wore it, too.

RENA: You never wore this.

NED: Daddy beat me up for it.

RENA: Oh, he did not. He never laid a finger on you. How can you say such an awful thing? How about giving us one tiny little bit of credit while I'm still alive.

NED: Mom... aren't you afraid of dying?

(HANNIMAN *comes in to take a sample of* NED's *blood.*)

RENA: Of course I'm frightened. Who isn't? What time is it? My friends are throwing me a farewell party. I see your brother left without saying goodbye. It's as if he's punishing me. He thinks I never notice. You think I don't know how you both treat me with such disdain? So many of my friends have kids who never see them at all. So I guess I must consider myself fortunate. You'll never guess what happened. I called Drew Keenlymore! He's listed in Vancouver. His very first words to me were, "My dear, I called every Weeks in the New York directory trying to find you." He tried to find me. He tried to find me. (*Re:* HANNIMAN.) What is she doing?

NED: A blood test.

RENA: Is my son going to be all right?

NED: My mother, Mrs. Weeks. Nurse Hanniman.

HANNIMAN: What a kind, pleasant, thoughtful, considerate son you have. I'm so enjoying taking care of him.

NED: Nurse Hanniman and I enjoy a rare bonding.

(HANNIMAN *leaves.*)

Momma... you may outlive me.

RENA: Don't say that. My momma was ninety-five years old when she died. She was withered beyond recognition. She was in a crib, mewling, wetting her pants, not knowing anyone, and me trying not to vomit from the putrid smell of urine and her runny stools. She simply would not let go. This old people's home had taken her every last cent for this tiny crib, for no nurse to come and wipe her. I wiped her. I came every day. I sat beside her. She didn't know who I was. My own mother. I'll bet you won't do all that for me. People stick articles under my door. "Your son's sick with that queer disease." "I saw your pervert son on TV saying homosexuals are the same as everyone else." Then, in our current events class we had a report on all the progress that's been made and how much your activists had to do with it and all the women came over and congratulated me. I don't know why, after ninety years, I'm surprised by anything.

NED: There hasn't been any progress.

RENA: Of course there has. Alexander...

NED: Yes, Momma?

RENA: He's dead. Drew Keenlymore is dead. I planned a trip to British Columbia, to Banff and Lake Louise, and I called to let him know I was going to be in the vicinity and he's gone and died. I guess we couldn't expect him to wait around for me forever, could we?

NED: No, Momma. I'm sorry.

RENA: Goodbye, darling. It's a long trip back. And I'm having trouble with my tooth. Every time I say goodbye I'm never sure I'm going to see you again. Give me a kiss.

(*They kiss.* NED *hugs her as best he can with his arms connected to the tubing.*)

NED: (*As she begins to leave.*) I wouldn't be a writer if you guys hadn't done what you did.

RENA: Is that something else I'm meant to feel guilty for?

NED: I love being a writer.

RENA: At last.

(RENA *walks off, slowly, holding on to things. She is almost blind.*

HANNIMAN *enters, with* DR. DELLA VIDA, *no longer in official uniform, and takes another blood test.*)

NED: Another one? Why am I having another one so quickly? What happened at the White House? What did *he* say?

TONY: They're cutting our budget.

NED: Your buddy. Is it too pushy of me to inquire as to my and/or your progress?

TONY: We have a fifty-fifty chance.

NED: That's your idea of progress?

TONY: You're not only pushy, you're... how do your people say it—a kvetch? Just imagine this is the cure and you're the first person getting it.

NED: Can I also imagine the Republicans never being re-elected?

HANNIMAN: He'd never work again.

TONY: Oh, I'll find a way. (*Leaves.*)

NED: Did the mouth of Weeks cause a little friction in the house of Della Vida?

HANNIMAN: Congratulations. You're my last patient.

NED: Where are you going?

HANNIMAN: To raise my baby. And be a pushy kvetch wife.

NED: How come?

HANNIMAN: It's somebody else's turn now. I think you can identify with that.

NED: Good luck.

HANNIMAN: You, too. Sweet dreams.

(*She turns out the lights and leaves.*

Darkness. NED *is tossing and turning.*)

NED: (*Screaming out.*) Ben!

BEN: (*Lying on a cot next to him.*) I'm here, Ned.

NED: Ben?

BEN: Yes, Ned.

NED: I'm scared.

BEN: It's all right. Go to sleep.

NED: Ben, I love you.

BEN: I love you, too.

NED: I can't say it enough. It's funny, but life is very precious now.

BEN: Why's it funny? I understand, and it is for me, too. A colleague of mine with terminal cancer went into his bathroom last week and blew his brains out with a shotgun.

(Dawn is breaking outside. BEN *gets up. He throws some cold water on his face at the sink.)*

NED: Hey, cheer me up, Lemon.

BEN: They haven't struck us out yet.

NED: What if this doesn't work?

BEN: It's going to work. *(Sits beside him on bed.)*

NED: Even if it does, it will only work for a while.

BEN: Then we'll worry about it in a while.

NED: You've certainly spent a great deal of your life trying to keep me alive, and I've been so much trouble, always trying to kill myself, asking your advice on every breath I take, putting you to the test endlessly.

BEN: I beat you up once.

NED: You beat me up? When?

BEN: We were kids. I was trying to teach you how to tackle in football. You were fast, quick. I thought you could be a quarterback. And you wouldn't do it right. You didn't want to learn. It was just perversity on your part. So I decided to teach you a lesson. I blocked you and blocked you, as hard as I could, much harder than I had to. And then I tackled you, and you'd get up and I'd tackle you again, harder. You just kept getting up for more. I beat you up real bad.

NED: I guess they want you to admit you don't know what the fuck's going on and go back to the drawing board. I'm worse? I'm worse!

TONY: Yes.

NED: What are you going to do?

TONY: There's nothing I can do.

NED: What do you mean there's nothing you can do? You gave me the fucking stuff! You must have considered such a possibility! You must have some emergency measures!

TONY: Oh, shut up! I am sick to death of you, your mouth, your offspring! You think changing Presidents will change anything? Will make any difference? The system will always be here. The system doesn't change. No matter who's President. It doesn't make any difference who's President! You're scared of dying? Let me tell you the facts of life: it isn't easy to die: you don't die until you have tubes in every single, possible, opening and orifice and vent and passage and outlet and hole and slit in your ungrateful body. Why, it can take years and years to die. It's much worse than you can even imagine. You haven't suffered nearly enough. (*Leaves.*)

NED: (*Pulls the tubes from his arms. Blood spurts out. Gets out of bed.*) What do you do when you're dying from a disease you need not be dying from? What do you do when the only system set up to save you is a pile of shit run by idiots and quacks? (*Yanks the tubes violently out of the wall apparatus, causing blood to gush out. Then pulls out the six bags of blood, smashing them, one by one, against the walls and floor, to punctuate the next speech.*)

My straight friends ask me over and over and over again: Why is it so hard for you to find love? Ah, that is the question, answered, I hope, for you tonight. Why do I never stop believing this fucking plague can be cured!

ALEXANDER: (*Appearing in the bath towels he was first seen in.*) What's going to happen to me?

NED: You're going to go to eleven shrinks. You won't fall in love for forty years. And when a nice man finally comes along and tries to teach you to love him and love yourself, he dies from a plague. Which is waiting to kill you, too.

ALEXANDER: I'm sorry I asked. Do I learn anything?

NED: Does it make any sense, a life? (*Singing.*) "Only make believe I love you..."

ALEXANDER: (*Singing.*) "Only make believe that you love me..."

NED: When Felix was offered the morphine drip for the first time in the hospital, I asked him, "Do you want it now or later?" Felix somehow found the strength to answer back, "I want to stay a little longer."

NED and ALEXANDER: "Might as well make believe I love you..."

NED: "For to tell the truth..."

NED and ALEXANDER: "I do."

NED: I want to stay a little longer.

THE END